PRAYER ANSWERED FOR PEGGY

By

DOROTHY MARTIN

MOODY PRESS
CHICAGO

Library of Congress Cataloging in Publication Data

Martin, Dorothy McKay, 1921-
  Prayer answered for Peggy.

  SUMMARY: When tragedy strikes Peggy's family,
prayer effects many changes for the better.

  [1. Prayers—Fiction]. I. Title.

PZ7.M35682Pr   [Fic]   75-45474

ISBN 0-8024-7610-4

Contents

1

Bad News

FOR PEGGY the flight home from California was only a string of names from a grade school social studies book—Denver, St. Louis, Chicago, Cincinnati. They were only words to her which showed that they were getting closer to home and to the news that Bob's phone call would bring about her father and Bill.

As they left the plane and quickly walked the length of the terminal, Uncle Walter said, "Wait here while I see about the baggage. Then we'll take a taxi and get out to the house as fast as possible."

The half-hour trip from the airport seemed endless to Peggy as they wove in and out of Sunday evening traffic. She was acutely conscious of her mother sitting erect beside her in the back seat, not speaking, not seeming to be aware of all that was going on. As the cab driver slowed, looking for the house, and turned into the driveway, a slight figure came from the early darkness of the porch and walked down the steps and across the grass.

"Alice! How come you're here? How did you know we were coming?" Peggy jumped out of the taxi as she spoke.

"Bob called before I went to church. He thought it might help if I were here when you got home so it wouldn't seem so—so lonely for you."

"But he didn't know what time we'd be here. Have you just been sitting here all alone waiting?"

Alice nodded. "I didn't mind," she answered simply. "I just wanted to be sure I was here when you came."

She stooped to pick up Peggy's train case, her long soft hair falling forward to hide her face. Peggy had seen her cover her face that way many times, through the years, when Alice knew something she didn't want to talk about.

"How come he called you? What did he tell you?" Peggy heard her voice sound loud and sharp with fear.

Before Alice could answer, the faint sound of a ringing phone came from inside the house. Uncle Walter called from the porch where he had helped the cab driver carry the suitcases. "We'd better answer that. Give me your key, Peggy."

She fumbled in her bag and dug it out, her fingers shaking as she handed it to him.

"You answer the phone," Uncle Walter ordered, when he had the door open. "I'll help your mother in." He turned to Mrs. Andrews, his voice gentle. "Come, Elizabeth."

Peggy pushed into the coolness of the shut-up house and reached to answer the insistent ring. It was Bob, as she had expected, and in answer to his question, she said, "We just this minute got here. Please, tell us everything. How is Bill? Is Dad all right? What happened?"

"I can't really give you any news about Bill. They've had him in surgery. He's out now, but they won't let me see him."

"Is he hurt badly?"

Bob's voice was low and troubled. "I just don't know, Peggy. I rode to the hospital in the ambulance; but Bill was unconscious, so I don't know how bad he was hurt. There may have been internal injuries—"

"But didn't the doctor tell you anything—"

"I haven't seen the doctor," he broke in. "No one tells me anything. They just brush past me as though I'm not even there! But I thought I should call you anyway, because I knew you'd be—wondering about—"

He stopped, his voice hanging in midair as though he didn't know how to finish the sentence.

Peggy forced out the question that had sat in her mind all the way across the country, the question she dreaded to ask because she feared the answer. "How—how is Dad? Is he with Bill?"

Bob's voice was husky as he answered. "Alice is there. She promised she would be. I'll hold on while she tells you."

Peggy turned to look her mute question across the room at Alice, who nodded the answer, her expressive face shadowed with sympathy. Her words came quickly.

"Bob said it happened so fast, Peggy. He had just finished his turn driving and was lying down in the back seat. He thinks that's what kept him from getting hurt. Your father was driving, and Bill was sitting beside him looking at the map. The man in the other car came the wrong way getting onto the highway. Your dad tried to get out of his way, and the car went off the road. It—turned over."

She stopped. The room was quiet except for the faint, metallic sound of Bob's voice at the other end of the line. The receiver was heavy in her hand, and she was hardly conscious of Uncle Walter taking it from her and talking briefly to Bob. Though she had expected this news, the certainty of it brought an unbearable sense of loss.

Her uncle turned from the phone, sorrow making his

voice sound tired. "Bob has been checking plane schedules
for us and says there are several possibilities yet tonight. He
will meet us in Louisville. If we can get on a flight tonight,
we'd better take it." He stopped and looked at Peggy and
then put his arm around her as he said gravely, "My dear,
I am sorry."

Peggy looked past him to her mother, who stood by the
wide front window, one hand on the back of the big, com-
fortable chair where her father had so often sat. She looked
up at her uncle, pain in her eyes. "How can I tell her?"

"Perhaps it's best not to say anything for the present.
That is, unless she asks a direct question."

Peggy nodded. She was so oppressed by what waited at
the end of this next part of the journey that she almost
wished she could shut it out of her mind the way her mother
had done.

"I promised to call Aunt Emily—"

"I'll do it, but first I want to check the flights to Louisville and try to get us on a plane tonight."

As her uncle dialed, Peggy turned to feel her way blindly
to her room and sink down on the bed, her face buried in
her hands. The anguish of her father's death submerged
every other thought and emotion. What would they do
without him? And if Bill were to—

She pushed the thought away and got up to walk back
and forth across the room, her hands gripped together. She
could only say over and over, "God—please help us—
please help us," unable to put the desolation of her feelings
into words.

She heard the soft knock on the door and looked around
as Alice opened it. "Your uncle got reservations, and you'll
have to leave right away."

Alice stood in the doorway, one hand on the doorknob,

and all their years of friendship stretched between them as they looked at each other across the width of the room. Peggy forced words past the full feeling in her throat.

"Thanks for being here, Alice. I just feel so—lost." She threw her hands out in a helpless gesture.

"If I can do anything at all, you know I will. Dan will hate not being here."

"I know. He wrote about his construction job, so I knew he wouldn't be in town. But he needs the money. I'll write—or call you. It just depends on how things are there."

* * *

Again time and place blurred as the plane burst up over clouds and then seemed to descend almost immediately. Bob hurried to meet them as they walked toward the information desk in the Louisville airport.

"Peggy, I can't tell you how sorry I am." He stopped, his voice choked.

He shook hands when Peggy introduced him to Uncle Walter and then looked at Mrs. Andrews as she stood silently in the bustle of the airport.

"How is she taking it?" he asked in a low voice.

"Ever since your telegram came, she's been the way you see her now. Sort of in shock, I guess. We don't think she really understands yet what's happened. Especially to Dad."

Peggy bit hard on her lower lip to stop its trembling. "Where is he?"

"At the funeral parlor in the town, which is about twenty miles from here. The accident happened on the other side of that town, and they rushed Bill there since it had a hospital. A specialist from a hospital here in Louisville is working with him. They took your dad there and are waiting for you to come and make arrangements. I thought you would probably want to take him home," he finished, his sympathy showing plainly on his face.

Peggy looked helplessly at her mother's empty face and then up at her uncle.

"You'll have to make the decision, I'm afraid," he answered the question in her look.

"Yes. Yes, I'm sure Mother will want to take him back home. He should be where his friends are and not—not down here all alone."

Tears blinded her eyes as she let Bob take her arm and lead her out to the parking lot with her mother and Uncle Walter following.

"I got you rooms at the little motel in town instead of here in Louisville, because I didn't think you'd want to drive back and forth every day. I thought we'd go to the hospital for a few minutes. It's late, and of course Bill won't be awake, but they said you could see him for a few minutes."

"Awake?" Peggy repeated. "That means he's been sleeping?"

"Not—exactly. He's not been conscious since the accident. I really can't tell you any more than that, Peggy. I'd better let you hear it from the doctor. I might say it the wrong way and give you the wrong impression just because I don't know how to explain what's wrong with him."

"You sound as though it—it could be— He *is* going to be all right, isn't he?"

Peggy's voice pleaded for reassurance, but Bob only shook his head. "I just don't know, Peggy. They had to operate. Something about pressure on the brain. And some vertebrae were damaged. I know it's serious, but that's all I know."

Peggy was aware then of the difference in the car they were in. "This isn't ours."

He shook his head. "It was completely smashed, Peggy. It's a miracle any of us came out alive. I'm just sorry we all didn't. Your father was such a great guy. Being with him and Bill this last month—I can't tell you what it did for me." His voice was somber, and his hands tightened on the steering wheel.

Peggy turned to stare out the window. She couldn't help the question that beat insistently. Why Dad? Why had this happened to him?

They drove the rest of the way in silence, following the winding mountain road to the outskirts of the little town and through the narrow, dark streets to the hospital entrance. The quiet darkness was broken only by an occasional bird chirping a protest at their noise. They followed Bob into the hospital and listened as he spoke to the nurse on duty at the desk. She nodded at his question and led the way up to the second floor where she stopped before a door with a No Visitors sign.

"The doctor left word you could see him just for a moment," she said softly. "But, please, don't try to speak to him."

She opened the door and stood aside for them to enter. Uncle Walter motioned Peggy and her mother inside, while he and Bob waited in the doorway. By the dim, shaded light over the bed, Peggy looked down at Bill's motionless figure, his face partly obscured by the bandages swathing his head. The few freckles across his nose stood out sharply against the whiteness of his skin.

From beside her, Peggy heard her mother say quietly, "He's sleeping so soundly."

Her voice was so calm in its whisper that Peggy caught her breath as she looked at her.

She really thinks he's just asleep! And she hasn't said anything about Dad! Peggy's uneasiness grew. How would her mother react when she came out of this state of shock?

The nurse came back into the room and motioned, and they turned obediently and followed her out. Bob drove them to the motel on the other side of the brief business district.

Peggy slept more soundly than she had expected to, exhausted by the emotional strain of the day. When she awoke and looked around the unfamiliar room, memory brought back all that had happened. Yesterday she had wakened to the bright California sun and the anticipation of Sally's coming to church. Today—she closed her eyes against the pain of the day with the decisions she had to make about Dad. Once again the only words she could form into a prayer were a plea for help.

They had little appetite for the weak coffee and day-old sweet rolls the smudged breakfast menu offered in the motel's tiny coffee shop. Bob drove them to the funeral parlor. Swallowing the tears that filled her throat, Peggy stepped inside after her mother and uncle. How could she possibly stand beside Dad's coffin and look at his still face and know his wit and love and understanding were gone from her forever? She closed her eyes to shield the tears, and from behind her came Mrs. Parker's familiar voice.

"Peggy, we came as soon as we heard."

She turned, startled, and Mr. Parker took her hand in his firm grip.

"How did you know?"

"Bob called us. We made unbelievable connections from Canada. We rented a car in Louisville and got here a few minutes ago. We have to go back on an early plane in the morning, but we had to come to see if we could help."

Peggy looked toward the room at the end of the hall. "Have you—seen him?"

"His body only, Peggy, not him. Remember, he's with the Lord in the great company of the redeemed." Mrs. Parker smiled at Peggy, though tears glistened in her eyes. She slipped her arm through Peggy's and reached a hand to Mrs. Andrews. "Come with me," she said and walked with them along the tiled hall.

Peggy looked down at her father's rested face and knew her tears were not for him but for her loss. She looked at her mother, who was staring down at the casket, and saw her face crumple as understanding brought tears.

"He's dead, then." Her voice trembled with the words, but there was acceptance of the fact, and Peggy felt some of the anxiety lift.

She wanted to say, "No, Mother, he's alive." But though it was true, her own feeling of loss was so great she knew she could not make the words sound convincing to her mother.

They stood in silence until Mrs. Andrews turned abruptly, shielding her face with one hand, and walked back to the door. Mrs. Parker followed her, stopping for a moment to look back over her shoulder at Peggy. "I'll stay with her while you make arrangements here."

Peggy turned to her uncle with a worried frown. "I hate to decide anything without asking Mother first. But you see how she is. Even though she finally seems to realize that Dad is—gone—" Peggy swallowed at the lump in her throat that made her voice come out high and thin.

"Let me ask if we can wait another day before making

a final decision," her uncle suggested. "Perhaps by then we'll have some definite word about Bill to help us know what direction to go."

It was Bill who occupied their thoughts. They were allowed to see him again briefly in the afternoon, and Peggy stood with her mother, watching him. His shallow breathing was all that showed he was alive.

They went to the hospital early the next morning, standing anxiously at the desk while the nurse checked the doctor's schedule.

"The patient was more restless last night than he has been. He hasn't regained consciousness yet, but he is definitely more alert than when he was brought in. After the doctor has seen him, he will be able to tell you more."

They trailed each other into the small waiting room. Peggy sat on the edge of the chair ready to jump when the doctor came. Mrs. Andrews sat, her back straight, her hands folded tightly together, staring straight ahead. Peggy looked at her anxiously, wishing she knew what her mother was thinking. It worried her that they had not talked at all. Both nights her mother had gone to bed and apparently fallen asleep immediately. She had not asked any questions or said anything about the accident. This had always been her defence against unpleasantness, Peggy knew—accepting it, but using it to build a shell of resentment and bitterness around herself. But this time the shell would have to be shattered eventually.

As she thought of her father gone, of Bill lying unconscious with his future uncertain, Peggy wondered how she could possibly say, "God's ways are perfect," and expect her mother to believe it. This would only make her turn scornfully from any talk of His goodness.

She thought of Aunt Emily's words just before they had

left California. "This doesn't change our prayers for your mother at all." The words rang hollow in the face of this enormous tragedy. Even she, knowing God, could not stop the questions that slipped through her mind. Why had God let it happen?

She looked up as the doctor strode toward them, frowning slightly. He looked around at them, his face serious. "You've got a very lucky young man in there. By all the statistics, he should be dead from the injuries he sustained and the time that elapsed before he was brought in."

"Does that—mean—he's going to b-be all right?" Peggy's fingers clutched the strap of her purse, and her voice quavered as she asked.

The doctor hesitated. "I can't answer a definite yes. I hope so. He's not conscious yet, but he seems more alert—his vital signs are encouraging. He fractured several vertebrae, which has left him paralyzed from the neck down. I must tell you in all honesty that he may go home in a wheel chair and never leave it. On the other hand, there is a chance that the paralysis will not be permanent. If—when he begins to recover, it will be slow. How well he does depends on many factors—how much grit he has—" He stopped and looked around at them. "And how much encouragement you give him."

"Don't worry about him," Bob exclaimed, his voice loud with relief that there was hope. "Bill's got plenty of grit."

"Good. He'll need it all." The doctor looked at them thoughtfully, studied Mrs. Andrews' face, and then looked at Uncle Walter.

"You are?"

"The boy's uncle."

"May I speak with you for a moment?"

Peggy watched the two men walk along the hall and felt

a rush of relief that they had Uncle Walter's experience
and common sense to depend on. She saw the two men
stop and stand deep in conversation, Uncle Walter nodding
his head and replying to the doctor's words. She turned to
Bob in sudden panic.

"Do you suppose there's something about Bill he hasn't
told us? Something else that's wrong with him?"

"Oh, no. They're probably just discussing business de-
tails. You know, this is going to be expensive," he worried, his voice low to keep Mrs. Andrews from hearing.

Peggy nodded and whispered back, "But it will be worth
it if Bill only gets well!"

She watched the men turn and come back along the hall.
Her uncle smiled reassuringly and said, "Elizabeth, you and
Peggy may see Bill for five minutes, but you're not to ask
him questions if he wakens."

Mrs. Andrews nodded impatiently. "I've seen him
through sickness before," she answered, her voice sharp.

Peggy saw the doctor frown as he started to speak and
then closed his lips in a tight, disapproving line. He was
obviously irritated, but Peggy could have shouted with relief. This was more like her mother. For her, a sharp
tongue was more natural than the apathy she had shown.

They followed the doctor's quick stride to Bill's room,
where he pushed open the door and motioned them in.
The nurse on duty stepped out of the room as Peggy walked
with her mother to the bed and looked down at Bill. The
other brief times they had seen him, she had only been conscious of his white face and the fact that he was at least
alive. Now she looked more closely at the bandages that
covered his head and shoulders and arm, and at the bottle
of intravenous solution that nourished him as he lay un-

conscious. Were his legs injured too? She wanted to reach out and feel them but was afraid to.

She watched her mother reach gently to curl her fingers around Bill's one unbandaged hand, which lay limp and defenseless on top of the sheet. She listened, startled, as her mother said softly, "He's not going to have you, Bill. He has your father, but I'm not going to let Him have you, too."

Her voice was determined and her face defiant as she lifted her head and looked steadily at Peggy.

2

Uncle Walter's Offer

UNCLE WALTER had waited outside Bill's room and walked with them down the stairs and along the hall.

"We'll have to make some decisions, Elizabeth," he said gently. "I'm thinking especially about the funeral arrangements. For John," he added unnecessarily.

Mrs. Andrews nodded. "He must be taken home. I can't think of his lying here, buried among strangers."

"I'll have Bob check plane reservations for us."

"But what about Bill?" Peggy protested. "He's not conscious—he can't be moved—"

"I shall stay here with him."

Peggy jerked around at her mother's words. "But—"

She stopped as she saw the slight shake of her uncle's head. Her mother's lips were fixed in that thin line which meant she had made her decision and would not change.

But surely she wants to go back with Dad, be with him to the end! Peggy stared at her mother's white, strained face, trying to will her to show some emotion. She couldn't say anything aloud, not in front of Bob or even Uncle Walter. There was too much unresolved family conflict that would unravel if one thread was pulled.

As they went down the hospital steps, Uncle Walter said softly, "Let us drop you and your mother at the funeral home, and you may have a chance to talk to her. I'll help make arrangements, but I think you two need a chance to talk things over privately."

Peggy was grateful for his understanding. "Mother didn't mean it the way it sounded. It's not that she doesn't want to be with Dad." She stopped, not sure herself how to explain it all.

He patted her arm. "Don't be upset, my dear. We all react to sorrow differently. And there is much in your mother's past that explains her feelings."

Later, as they waited for Bob to come back for them, Mrs. Andrews said abruptly, "You may find my attitude hard to understand, Peggy, but this is the way I feel, and I can't pretend otherwise. Your father—he insisted on coming here— If he had stayed home— If he—had not c-come—"

Her voice had been firm and steady but now was ragged. As Peggy reached a sympathetic hand, her mother straightened and lifted her chin. "Now that he is gone, there is nothing more I can do for him. He is gone. But Bill is here and needs my help. My place is with him, and I will stay until he is well or until he can be moved home."

"But where will you stay? It may be a long time."

"I'll stay at the motel for now. Later I'll look for a room somewhere that will be less expensive."

"There may not be any. This is such a small town."

"There'll be something. Someone surely would like to rent out a bed. I will only need a place to sleep, since I'll be with Bill most of the time. I can probably have my meals at the hospital. When Bill can be released— Well, we'll make plans as they are needed."

"But Mother—"

"Please don't argue with me, Peggy. I've made my decision, so there is no point in discussing it further."

When Uncle Walter heard of her plan, he shook his head doubtfully. "I'd feel better if you'd stay on at the motel. Let me help with the expense—"

"No!" Then her voice softened a little. "You've done enough, Walter, coming with us as you have. I appreciate your concern, but I'm used to doing things my own way, and I want to continue. Especially now that I—that I am alone." She stopped to steady her voice. "If it will make you feel more at ease, I'll promise to ask you for help if I need it. Until then, please let me manage my affairs as I think best."

"But there are other things we haven't even talked about," Peggy broke in. "I can't just go off to college as though nothing has happened and leave you here alone."

"Certainly you can. There's no reason at all for you to change your plans. It would mean losing out on your scholarship. I'll be all right, if you will all please let me work things out my own way."

Uncle Walter shook his head at Peggy when she started to protest, and said, "At least we will drive around with you and see what is available."

It didn't take long to drive through the town. Peggy peered out at the narrow streets winding along the slopes of the wooded hills and a thin river, forded by an old covered bridge, threading its way along the south end of town. The beauty was lost on Peggy as she wondered how they could possibly find out who might want to rent out a room.

"We should stop and ask someone," she worried. "But these houses all look so small, there wouldn't be room—"

"Peggy, please! I will have plenty of time to look after you are gone. I'll inquire at the hospital. There will be something." Peggy heard the stubborn note in her mother's voice and knew it was useless to argue.

* * *

They stopped at the hospital on the way to the airport the next morning, and Peggy went to see Bill one more time, praying that a miracle had happened and he would be conscious. A slender young girl had just cleaned the room and was bringing a pitcher of cold water as they came through the door. She glanced at them and then quickly away. Then she looked at Bill and turned to Peggy with a shy smile.

"He is your brother?"

Peggy nodded, seeing the wide-set blue eyes and hearing the slight hesitation in her speech.

"I'm sorry he is hurt so bad. I hope he gets to feelin' all right." Her voice was soft and timid-sounding.

"Of course he will be all right," Mrs. Andrews broke in, her voice crisp. "Now if you are through, we'd like to be alone with him."

The note of abrupt dismissal was plain in her voice, and the girl awkwardly gathered up her cleaning supplies and backed out of the room, not looking at them.

Bill lay motionless, the sheet lifting and falling with his quiet breathing. Peggy looked down at him and then across at her mother. "I wish there were something I could do. I hate to leave you alone."

"I have nothing better to do with my time than help Bill recover."

"I know. But—it's just that I feel so selfish going on with my life as though nothing were wrong when Bill is—is like this." She stopped and caught her lower lip between her teeth to stop its trembling. "It doesn't seem fair to him."

"There is nothing you could do for him by staying here.
You would only miss out on your opportunities. You
worked hard for this chance for college. It is too bad that
Bill must miss several months of school. But he will make
it up quickly. He can go to summer school to make up the
work he misses this fall and be ready for college next year,
just as he had planned."

Mrs. Andrews' voice was brisk and assured, and Peggy
wondered how she could ignore the possibility that Bill
might never go to school again. Then she saw her mother's
fingers pleating and unpleating the edge of the sheet and
knew she did not feel as confident as she sounded. Then
her mother looked at her across the width of the bed.

"I'm letting you get off to college by yourself. I'm sorry.
But—" She stopped and reached a hand toward Peggy in a
pleading gesture. "Don't you see? Bill needs me right now
more than you do. Just close and lock the house, and go on
with your plans. You have church friends who will help
you."

Peggy lifted her head in surprise at the note of momentary
wistfulness in her mother's voice. But then Mrs. Andrews
went on in her usual controlled tone.

"I'll let you know how things develop here, and of course
I will bring Bill home at the earliest opportunity."

Peggy stood silent, tracing her finger along a crease in
the light blanket folded across the foot of the bed. Was her
mother just going to ignore the funeral service she would
face back home? As though reading her thoughts, Mrs.
Andrews turned and walked over to look out the window,
her back to Peggy.

"I've talked to your uncle, and he is going to stay with
you until John—your father—is—is buried." Her voice
broke, and her face crumpled as she turned to Peggy. She

wiped at the tears on her cheeks as she said, "I just c-can't f-forgive him for doing this."

Peggy put her arms around her and patted her back silently, not sure whether it was God or her father who was meant. She listened as her mother's voice went on.

"I'm not hard or unfeeling, Peggy. I know people will misunderstand if I don't come up with you for the funeral. But I keep thinking Bill might regain consciousness and I would not be here. Or he might—he might—"

She stopped and turned away again. In a voice taut with controlled emotion she finished, "Someone must be here at this crucial time. I don't think it wise for me to leave even long enough to fly home and right back. Your father does not need me any longer, but Bill does."

"I suppose you're right. If you left and Bill wanted you— But call the minute there is any change."

* * *

Peggy had asked Mr. Parker to take care of all the arrangements for the funeral service, which was brief and simple. The church was crowded with the many friends who had come to share the sorrow and loss. Afterward, Peggy went home with Uncle Walter, and everything she saw brought memories of her father. Even the slightly crooked garage door was a reminder of the many times he had tried to jack it up and then had said ruefully, "How can anyone who is intelligent enough to understand the directions for doing this, be so dumb when he tries to follow them?"

She sat down at the dining room table and dropped her head on her arms and cried. Uncle Walter stood by, patting her shoulder, then walked back and forth through the house, chewing at his lip thoughtfully.

Finally she straightened up, wiping her eyes. "I'm sorry.

All the lostness and the emptiness of no one being here hit
me all of a sudden.. And knowing Dad won't ever be
back—" She stopped, fighting for control while tears
brimmed her eyes again.

Then she begged, "Uncle Walter, is Bill *really* going to be
all right? Are you sure the doctor didn't tell you something
he didn't tell us?"

He pulled out a chair and sat down beside her. "Peggy,
we must have a serious talk about what's ahead for Bill
and your mother. If you won't think I'm interfering, I'd
like to go through your father's insurance policies and other
business papers. Your mother will consider any offer of
help to be interference. You and I know that. But she's
going to need help, regardless. She won't be able to manage the financial burden alone."

"But you know she'll want to get a job and be independent. I don't know how much insurance Dad had, but
Mother can have it all. I won't have any expenses at college because of my scholarship—except personal needs.
I'm sure Bill will get a scholarship, too."

She watched her uncle stand up and walk to the window
to stare out into the summer haze. Finally he turned and
looked at her.

"You asked what the doctor told me. I'll give it to you
straight. Bill is the problem."

"What do you mean?"

"The doctor said he will live. There's no question about
that. But his recovery will be slow and expensive. He'll
need therapy for a long time."

"Because of the paralysis? But—he will get over it,
won't he?" Peggy looked at her uncle's troubled face and
watched him slowly shake his head.

"The doctor thinks it likely—not definite, but likely—

that Bill will have some permanent paralysis. He's not prepared to say to what extent."

Peggy closed her eyes against the painful picture of active, energetic Bill dragging a crippled leg or limping haltingly on crutches or perhaps—perhaps not even walking at all. She listened numbly as her uncle went on.

"Don't give up hope, Peggy. The doctor admitted that his diagnosis could be wrong, but he wanted to prepare us for what could happen. And of course, therapy can do a great deal to repair damaged muscles and nerves. Bill's own determination will be a big factor in his recovery. Then, too, you and I are not forgetting God's power to work a miracle."

He stopped to put a comforting arm around her shoulders. Then he sat down across the table from her again.

"What I am thinking of primarily now is the expense your mother is facing. Expense she may not have thought of yet. You know something of the situation between your aunt and mother. There has been this underlying antagonism for many years. Some of it is justified; some is not. But you also know that your aunt and I have been drastically changed by God. We feel that, since we are Christians, we owe your mother a tremendous debt. Right now there doesn't seem to be any way we can reach her. You saw that in your visit with us this past month. But something we can do is pay Bill's hospital expenses. That is, any that are not covered by insurance."

"But Mother won't—"

"I know she won't willingly accept any help. But I've made arrangements with the doctor and the hospital to forward bills to me and just tell her they are cared for. She won't like it but—" He stopped, shrugging his shoulders. Then with a crooked grin he added, "Perhaps we'd better pray that God will soften her attitude about this. I certainly do not want to antagonize her needlessly. If she can see it's more for Bill's sake than her own, it will be easier for her to accept the help."

Peggy reached to squeeze his hand. "How can we ever thank you!"

"There is no need for thanks." His voice was sad as he went on. "I must confess there was a time Emily and I would not have done this. Thank God He changed us in time."

He cleared his throat and went on in his usual crisp tone. "I want to make another suggestion to your mother, but I don't think she is ready for it yet. When Bill can be moved, instead of coming here, I'd like them to come to California. Bill can recuperate there, where he won't have to battle ice and snow. There's an excellent clinic near us, where he can get any therapy he needs. Your mother can make her home with us. Since you'll be in college, there's no need to keep this house. That's why I'd like to see your father's business papers and check the mortgage to see what can be done about selling—"

"No, wait!"

Through Peggy's mind flashed the image of her mother sitting at Aunt Emily's lovely table, being waited on by a uniformed maid, sleeping in Aunt Emily's beautiful guest room not even needing to make the bed, and all the time being gnawed by the envy and bitterness that had eaten at her for so long. No, the plan wouldn't work. The goal was to reach her mother, not drive her away.

As her uncle looked at her, surprised by the urgency of her voice, she pleaded, "Let's wait. Please? I know you want to help Mother, and I want you to. But I think we have to let her help herself. Uncle Walter, maybe I'm not saying this so you'll understand, but Mother's strong—a lot stronger than you realize. She can take an awful lot of disappointments, even if she doesn't always take them in the right way. She's got to be left alone to do all she can for herself."

She stopped for a moment, searching for the words to express the certainty that had come to her. "I think she has to come to the place where she absolutely can't help herself anymore. And where she finds other people can't help her either. Maybe—maybe then she'll break down and let God help her. Don't you think so?" she pleaded.

Her uncle stood, his lips pursed in thought, his fingers tapping the table. Then he nodded. "Yes, perhaps you are right. I've been rushing ahead with what I thought was the best solution, partly, I think, because it would be a way Emily and I could atone for the past. But perhaps my suggestion isn't the right one."

He smiled across at her. "Let's form a conspiracy. I'll pay some bills for her, just enough that she won't be swamped. But I'll leave enough so that she will see she can't be entirely independent from our help."

Peggy nodded, smiling back at him. "And then we'll pray that she will find even other people aren't enough— that she needs God too."

3

New Surroundings

AS THEY WAITED at the airport the next afternoon for his plane to leave, Uncle Walter looked anxiously at Peggy.

"Now, my dear, if you need anything at all, don't hesitate to let us know. Call collect at any time. After you've talked to your mother this evening, if there is anything we should know or anything we can do, be sure to call. Remember our pact." His eyes twinkled as he looked at her.

"I will. But don't worry about me. I'll just lock the house when I go. Alice's Dad said he would check it regularly to see that everything is all right."

"And you'll stay with them until you leave for school?"

"Yes, it's just for a couple of days. I go Monday. I'll send you my address as soon as I'm settled."

He looked at her thoughtfully. "It's been a long time since I was in college, and I suppose things are different now in some respects. But as I remember, one of the best parts was the fun and foolishness that went on. Get in on that, too, Peggy, in spite of the anxiety you'll have about Bill and your mother."

He smiled at her, and Peggy smiled back, seeing the laugh lines crinkling the corners of his eyes. It was hard to remember that she had once been afraid of him, scared of the severity of his face.

"A lot will depend on Sarah Elizabeth Montgomery, I guess. My roommate," she explained to his puzzled look.

"That's a lot of name to carry around. Let us know if she lives up to it."

He picked up his small bag as his flight was called and then paused to look at her again. "My dear, I'm not particularly good at being a father, and of course I could never take the place of yours. But when you need to think of someone in that way, I would be honored if you chose me. We'll keep in close touch." He bent somewhat awkwardly and kissed her cheek.

The mist in her eyes blurred her vision as she watched him disappear from sight along the covered ramp leading to the plane. She walked slowly back through the crowd to where Bob and Alice waited in the car.

Alice looked at her questioningly when Bob pulled up in front of the house. "Do you want me to come help?"

"No thanks. I've got to sort some stuff and do some final packing. If it's all right with you, I won't come over until about nine tonight. I'll find stuff to eat, and then I'm going to call Mother about eight o'clock. See you later."

She went into the silent house, its emptiness an aching reminder of her loss. To keep from breaking down in tears again, she got the vacuum cleaner and dust cloths, and cleaned and polished, waxing the furniture in each room thoroughly. But when she got to her parents' room, the sight of her father's personal belongings brought such hurt that she closed the door on them. That room would have to wait until the pain had been eased by time.

She watched the clock, waiting for the hands to move around to eight, and then made herself wait until eight-thirty to give her mother time to get back to the motel. When she finally dialed the motel number there was no answer from her mother's room. She sat by the phone, worry building in her. It could simply mean that she was staying longer at the hospital than she had said she would, or that she had stopped to get something to eat. Or it could mean that Bill was—

She pushed the thought away and tried again, letting the phone ring repeatedly. She was just about to hang up when her mother's quick, "Hello?" carried to her.

"Hello, Mother! I'm so glad to hear your voice! How's Bill? . . . Just the same? Does the doctor think it's all right that there's no change? . . . You found a place to stay? Great! Where is it? . . . Sounds kind of far—No, I suppose not since the town is small. How did you get it? . . . No, I don't remember—oh, you mean the pretty girl who was cleaning the room. . . . Ellie? Her grandmother? . . . Have you seen the room? . . . I hope it will be all right. Mother, I just wish you weren't there all alone!"

She knew her voice sounded worried and wistful, and she listened to her mother's quick, vigorous reassurance. "Don't even think about me, Peggy. I'm just where I should be and where I want to be. I've seen the room; and, while it is small and rather sparsely furnished, it will suit my purpose very well. I'll be with Bill most of each day and will only be in the room to sleep. That way I won't see much of my landlady. I'm afraid she's the type who will be somewhat of a busybody if I give her any opportunity. I'll write you and describe my situation in more detail soon. There's no need whatever for you to worry about me."

"You'd better give me your phone number there. At the house where you're staying I mean."

"I can't. There is no phone there. But it doesn't matter." Her tone was crisp. "There's no need to spend money making phone calls. If there is urgent news, I'll get in touch with you at school as soon as I have your number."

"Uncle Walter wants you to call them, too."

No answer came for a moment, and then she answered, "If there's any need."

Peggy waited, hoping her mother would ask a question. When she did not, she said slowly, "Mother, lots of people came to the service yesterday. And everyone said to tell you how s-sorry they are."

She could hear her mother's quickened breathing in the slight pause between them, and then she answered, "I was there in thought with you, Peggy, sharing the sorrow. I sat with Bill, though he was not aware of it, and thought of you. I was glad you had friends with you to make it a little easier." Her voice trembled as she finished and then as they said goodbye.

Peggy slowly put down the receiver and stood looking around the quiet room, at the shadows that filled it, shrouding its familiarity. Loneliness swept over her, and she swallowed at the tears that persisted in welling up. She felt like a child away from the safety of home for the first time and longing for the comfort of family. But her family was shattered, and she had never felt so alone.

Then came a slight sound, the click of the screen door opening, and Alice called softly, "Peggy, are you about ready?"

They clung together for a moment, and Peggy said, "Alice, you're always here just when I need you. You always have been all these years."

"Well, God made friends to help, didn't He?"

They stood smiling at one another in the soft darkness of the room and Peggy's lonely feeling faded. The years fell away to that awful time when she had moved to town as a shy, self-conscious seventh-grader, eagerly grateful for the friendship Alice had given right from the start. How

close they had been through the years. They could talk
about anything and laugh together—or cry. And Alice was
always the same, always a friend. How many experiences
they had shared, and how deep their friendship had grown.
It was there strengthening them both, even when they were
separated.

For that moment, Peggy felt as though she would like to
brace herself and hold back the hours that were rushing at
her to take her away from the safe familiarity of people and
places she knew and into the new and strange.

But that was not possible. And there was an undeniable
excitement about going to college and getting on with the
new life that was opening to her. This anticipation helped
to mute the sorrow and take her over the parting with Alice
and other friends in church.

*   *   *

The certain conviction she had had that she would like
Sarah Elizabeth Montgomery was solidified as soon as
they met in the dorm lounge. Sarah was tall, with short,
curly hair, a wide smile that flashed a deep cleft in one
cheek, and gray eyes that said plainly, "Isn't life exciting?"

But even in the busy, hectic, fun week of freshman orien-
tation, Peggy's thoughts centered frequently in the small,
narrow-streeted, hilly town in Kentucky. Whenever she
thought of it, she despaired that her mother could be
reached in that setting, so different in background and culture from everything she valued. Still, Bill was there. And
if—no, *when* he recovered, that surely would be evidence
to her mother of God's love and concern for her.

She went to the mailbox on Friday and tore open the
letter that was there in her mother's precise, straight-lined
handwriting.

DEAR PEGGY,

You will want to know my address, now that I am settled. I cannot give you an exact house number, since this town is too small for street numbers. Everyone picks his mail up at the post office. You only need the town and state and zip number. In addition, put the letter in care of Mrs. Withrow. Everyone here calls her Grandma Withrow, but of course, I shall never do that.

She seems to know everyone and everyone's business, so I shall have to be on guard not to let her know mine and interfere.

She does have a clean house, and my room, though small, is adequate. It is upstairs over the kitchen and has a rocking chair, a narrow bed with an iron bedstead, and a dresser with two drawers and a mirror over it. They are old pieces, but if I am any judge they could be quite valuable, since they seem to have been handmade. Probably there is a story behind each piece, which my landlady would doubtless tell me if I gave her any opportunity—which I certainly shall not.

Thankfully, she is meticulously clean. She is poor and quite obviously needs the money I am paying for the room. I am able to eat my meals at the hospital since there is a cafeteria there, though from what I have observed and tasted thus far, the cook has very little imagination. There is also a small restaurant in town.

I have settled pretty much into a routine which will change as Bill's condition changes. I go to the hospital in the morning and stay with Bill until the middle of the afternoon. Then I walk back to my room for an hour or so before returning to the hospital for an early meal and to spend the evening with Bill. The cafeteria at the hospital closes early—as does the whole town, for that matter.

As to Bill's condition, there is not much to report that is new. He seems more restless each day, which the doctor keeps assuring me is a good sign. The doctor claims it is not unusual for a person to be unconscious for so long. I am with Bill as much as possible, for I do not want to miss the moment when he wakens.

The doctor will show me how to assist with massage and other therapy when he is able to have it. Having something definite to do will be less wearing than this waiting.

You know my feelings about prayer, Peggy. I cannot in good conscience beg for favors from a God who would allow Bill to be hurt and your father killed. But since you do pray, there is something you should know. The doctor admitted to me today that there is a slight possibility that Bill could be handicapped mentally because of insufficient oxygen to the brain during the early moments of the injury. Since I am sure you will insist on praying and have been doing so, this is what you should be concerned about.

I have not talked about you and your situation, Peggy. It is not that I am not interested, as I am sure you know. But I am confident I need not worry about you. With your finances cared for and your good mind, you will do well in your college work. I'm sure your interest in church and your upbringing will keep you from the dangers that hit many young people when they go off to college.

Write as you have time. I will keep you informed as things progress here. There is not much of interest to write about except Bill, and just now there is nothing new to report. I will not be meeting people here socially, and certainly have no intention of letting anyone know of my affairs, particularly my landlady.

I experience a measure of loneliness, of course, but it is to be expected. It will be worth it when Bill recovers.

Much love,
MOTHER

Peggy reread the letter, an ache in her throat as the sound of her mother's voice came so clearly through the words. The reserve that was so much a part of her nature was evident in the letter's phrasing. Peggy knew it was the shield she had used through the years as a guard against what she considered to be sentimentality. And sometimes the shield seemed so hard.

Peggy tapped the letter on her desk and stared through the open window, hardly conscious of the warm fall breeze fluttering the curtains and carrying the sounds of laughter from the campus. If only her mother had found a room with someone who would be soft and understanding instead of this person whose snooping would antagonize.

"There *must* be a reason for it!"

She said the words aloud fiercely but with a hopelessness. How would her mother ever see in all this her need of God? She looked down at the letter again. Especially if it were true that Bill—that he might be mentally—No! She thrust the thought away. That would be so much worse even than physical paralysis. If all that had happened so far in her mother's life had turned her from God, how much more such a tragedy would.

The clock ticked away the afternoon as Peggy sat at her desk, praying for Bill's urgent need—and for her mother— and for herself to know what to write back.

She would have felt even more hopeless about the situation if she had seen her mother when she had finished

writing the letter. Mrs. Andrews had sealed it quickly and
put on the stamp and then sat looking around the small
room.

She had told Peggy the truth. It was clean. The wood
floor with its wide planks was almost white from frequent
scrubbing. The narrow window beside the bed let the sun
through its sparkling glass to reflect on the mirror above the
dresser. The small rocker with the wide-slatted back and
cane bottom creaked slightly every time it rocked back. It
brought a reminder of Mrs. Withrow's words when she had
showed the room. "A body needs to git rid of problems;
rockin' helps."

She knew she had not adequately described her surroundings to Peggy, but they were not important enough to
her to bother about. This was only a temporary stopping
place to be forgotten as soon as it was no longer needed.

She stood up abruptly and walked around the end of the
narrow bed with its handmade patchwork quilt to look out
the window. In the distance beyond were more hills like the
one against which the town was built and against which this
house stood—or rather, leaned. By craning her neck she
could see the outcropping of rock to the west of the house,
with the garden planted near it and yet far enough out to
catch the afternoon sun.

As she stood at the window, she saw Mrs. Withrow come
out to pick supper beans. Her head was bare, and the sun
glinted on the big, metal hairpin which was fastened
through the bun into which her thin gray hair was pulled
at the nape of her neck. Arthritis had crippled her, bending
her shoulders and thrusting her head forward so that she
looked up from under the thin line of her eyebrows.

Mrs. Andrews watched as she moved around the garden,
feeling for each bean and picking it carefully. What would

she have for supper? She tried to remember what she had read of this part of the country and of the customs of the people and what they ate. Beans and smoked ham? Biscuits and gravy? She found herself suddenly hungry and turned from the window restlessly, glancing at her watch. It was time to go to the hospital and have a tasteless meal in the cafeteria before going in to sit with Bill.

She washed her hands and face in the tiny bathroom next to her room and went down the steep stairs to the first floor. The stairway opened directly into the kitchen, which led out onto the porch. Though there was another entrance to the house, this one faced the road and was the one used most of the time.

Mrs. Withrow sat on a chair facing the row of colorful plants lining the porch railing, the pan of beans in her lap.

"You're goin' early today."

"A little. I want to walk around a bit."

"Not much to see in town. Oh, the scenery all over is purty enough. That part's been left the way God made it. Take yourself a short walk back around that road there." She gave a quick, jabbing nod at the road running in the opposite direction from town. "Makes you think about God back there in the quiet."

"Thank you, but I don't have that much time." Mrs. Andrews deliberately made her voice crisp. "I spend all the time I can with my son."

"Ellie says he's a right nice young fellow. Can't tell much, of course, with him just lyin' there. But he must be a fine boy for his people to care so much about him."

She paused and squinted her dark brown eyes up at Mrs. Andrews. "Too bad about the accident—to him and to your man. But then, we know God's doing is always best."

Anger rose in Mrs. Andrews at the words. It was bad

enough to be a prying old woman, but to be a pious snoop was worse. She stepped down off the porch to the ground and then stopped and looked back.

"I don't happen to believe that. God has taken my husband and left my son as he is. If this is the best He can do, He's not much of a God."

She turned without waiting for an answer and walked along the road that led into town, so blinded by anger that she was hardly conscious of the stores and houses that lined the one main street and branched off to follow footpaths down the sides of the hill. She knew the buildings were there, because she had passed them other days; but today her one thought was to leave Mrs. Withrow and her empty piety behind.

The hospital was at the far end of town, on the outskirts really, perched against the side of the hill and reached by a winding, gravel driveway. Mrs. Andrews wondered as she had each day she walked to it how this backward little town happened to have a hospital. The building had once been a shining white, but now the paint was weathering and peeling. The wide, shallow front steps sagged in the middle, and deep cracks ran the length of several of the steps.

The lobby was cool after the warmth of the fall sun, but she wrinkled her nose in distaste at the smell of cooking cabbage that drifted from the cafeteria at the back of the building. She had eaten there seven days, and this was the third time that particular menu was offered, if the cabbage smell meant that along with it the cook was serving spareribs, boiled potatoes, and rubbery jello.

Instead of going to the cafeteria as she had planned, she turned and went up the stairs to the second floor and along the hall to Bill's room, pushing the door open quietly. She stopped as she saw Ellie sitting in the chair by the bed, her eyes watching Bill as he lay motionless, his breath coming in slow, regular rhythm. Ellie's face was in profile, and Mrs. Andrews saw the slender cheekbone and the blond hair that waved back from her low forehead and fell down her thin back. It was not until she turned to look directly at a person and speak in a soft drawl in which the slurred syllables of the words were heard that it was clear the lovely face and bright smile hid a slow mind.

Ellie had not heard the door open; and, as Mrs. Andrews moved closer, she looked around, startled. She jumped up quickly, a shy smile curving her lips.

"Oh! I didn't hear you come in. I jest thought I'd sit a spell with him 'til you came. It would sure be wonderful to be here when he wakes up."

She looked at Mrs. Andrews questioningly. "If you haven't et, I kin stay some longer—"

Mrs. Andrews shook her head. "I'm not hungry. I will eat later."

"There ain't no place open later on."

"It doesn't matter." Mrs. Andrews didn't try to keep her impatience from showing. "Please, run along now."

The anger she had brought in with her still festered. The girl had no business taking such an interest in Bill. It was her job to clean and do whatever else was necessary, but to sit with Bill in her absence? No! She would put a stop to that.

Ellie understood the curt dismissal, for she colored and backed away, stumbling into a chair as she did so and then fumbling for the doorknob.

Mrs. Andrews moved the chair to the other side of the bed, somewhat shaken by the intensity of her feelings. She had perhaps been too sharp. The girl had meant no harm. She was probably intrigued by the atmosphere of mystery surrounding someone who lay motionless and yet who could waken at any time. She reached a hand to cover Bill's and sat still as the minutes moved by, memory bringing scenes from the past.

Lights came on in the hall as the shadows deepened outside and the chirping of the birds became less shrill. She reached finally to snap on the dim light at the side of Bill's bed and looked at him, trying to will his eyes to open and the familiar grin to light his face. But there was no response.

The night nurse came in to do the necessary things for him, and Mrs. Andrews stood. This was the signal to leave, though she did so reluctantly each night. She said the usual, "You'll send word if I'm needed?"

The nurse nodded. "I expect, though, that Grandma Withrow will know if there's a change almost as soon as we do. She's a wise, knowing old lady. You couldn't have found a better place to stay."

Mrs. Andrew's heels clicked down the stairs and out the door, tapping out her irritated thought. *What nonsense! She couldn't know unless she were told.*

She walked quickly down the gravelled driveway and toward the town, which had already settled for the night. A few lights showed here and there in tiny, winking gleams as though they were reflections of the stars which seemed close enough to touch. Away from the town the darkness was intense and the quiet so deep she could almost feel it. But it was a friendly darkness, and she felt no fear walking in it as she would have felt at home on the dark city streets.

The anger that had been in the back of her mind over Ellie and had flared at the nurse's remark was soothed by the deep silence and peace of her surroundings. By the time she turned in at the path leading from the road to the house and stepped on to the porch to enter the kitchen, she was aware only that she was hungry.

Mrs. Withrow turned from the stove at the sound of the screen door opening and looked across the room. Then she indicated the table, which was set with a plate and knife and cup.

"Ellie said you hadn't et. That ain't good when you're so rail thin. Set and have a cup of tea and some bread and tomato preserves. You'll sleep better."

Mrs. Andrews hesitated. Her desire for privacy was overshadowed by this simple gesture of hospitality, her impatience and anger at Ellie at odds with her hunger for food and companionship.

"Thank you. It's very kind of you. But I don't want to be a burden. Our agreement was only for the room, not for meals." She heard the stiff sound of her voice and knew it was partly regret that she had lashed out at Ellie and now was being repaid by kindness.

"This ain't no meal!" Mrs. Withrow's voice carried scorn as she answered. " 'Sides, I've seen what they feed people at that hospital. You'd need a good, strong cup of tea to settle your stomach if you *had* et up there."

Later, stretching out on the hard mattress with the rough sheet tucked up under her chin against the cool night air coming in the window, and prepared for the usual night of sleeplessness, Mrs. Andrews found herself unexpectedly drowsy and satisfied.

4

A Battle Won

THE UNUSUAL SENSE of peace was with her when she woke in the morning to the sound of birds starting the day early. She lay still, feeling rested as she had not felt since coming to this place, and thought through the routine of the day. The morning and early afternoon she would spend with Bill, take a break in the afternoon for a walk and a rest, then go back with Bill again until time for bed. She closed her eyes in pain against the thought that this could go on for months, or even years.

She pushed the thought away. No! Today she would ask the doctor what could be done to rouse Bill. Surely there was some treatment he could give that would bring Bill out of the suspended state he was in and start him toward recovery. Even if returning consciousness showed physical or mental disability, she could face that better than this uncertainty.

She threw back the sheet and got up to pull open the heavy door of the old-fashioned wardrobe cupboard that served as a closet. The house was quiet as she dressed. For the first time since moving in, she wondered whose room she was renting. She knew Mrs. Withrow slept downstairs in a room off the kitchen. She had heard someone moving around in the room next to hers early every morning and assumed it was Ellie. She turned to look around her. There were no personal items on the dresser top or in the drawers, no pictures, nothing to show that the room had once belonged to someone.

She shrugged and closed the door behind her and went down the steep stairs, not even glancing around the empty kitchen as she went through it. These people were none of her business. She did not want them prying into her affairs, and she certainly was not going to pry into theirs. But as she walked toward the hospital, Ellie's pretty young face, with its eagerness and shy warmth, nagged at her. Why was she living with her grandmother? Where were her parents? What future was there in a small, isolated town like this for a young girl, particularly one like Ellie who could not go on to school?

What was there to keep *anyone* in this place, she wondered as she looked around. What did people do for a living? Two women coming toward her along the sidewalk moved to one side to let her by, and she was sure they turned to stare after her as she passed them, curious about her. She walked on with her shoulders erect and her chin lifted, ignoring the glances and occasional nods of women hanging clothes to dry in the early morning sun.

Passing a grocery store, two gas stations, a hardware store, the post office, a boat rental agency, and a dozen or so small houses brought her to the edge of town and to the road that led up toward the hospital. She stopped and turned to look back over her shoulder. On the opposite end of the town was a church and the small motel. Other houses were dotted up and down the sides of the hill. *There must be a schoolhouse somewhere,* she thought idly as she stood looking around.

The wooded hills were beautiful in the sun's shimmering haze, which mingled with a thin mist rising lazily from the valley floor. Here and there leaves were beginning to turn color. Faint red and yellow shades among the green of most of the leaves made the view more like an oil painting on canvas than real life. A dog howled mournfully in the distance, but the sound was offset by the cheerful twittering of birds nearby.

She remembered how Bill had talked about the beauty of this part of the country when he was here last year. That was one reason he had come back this year and had talked his father into coming too.

Mrs. Andrews turned abruptly, pushing away the hurting thoughts, and walked rapidly up the sloping driveway to the hospital entrance. Her breath came in quick gasps as she reached the wide porch with its shallow, sagging steps. She pushed open the front door, answering with a brief nod the greeting of the nurse at the front desk, and walked quickly along the hall to the stairs and up to the second floor. Ellie was down at the far end of the floor with her cleaning cart, apparently not having gotten to Bill's room yet.

She opened the door quietly and went in. The eager hope that flared each time she entered the room died as she stood at the foot of the bed and looked down at Bill. He lay as he had all the days since the accident, his eyes closed, his breathing a regular, slow rhythm under the sheet. She crossed over to the window and pulled up the shade to let the sun light up the room, hoping it would lift the gloom she could feel settling over her. A breeze rustled in busily, billowing out the curtains and sweeping across the floor in little running gusts.

As she looked outside, the brightness was only for other people in happier situations. For her the day was only another long stretch of waiting, with no assurance that the waiting would end happily. She thought of Bill, of his eagerness and enthusiasm and delight in life. It was not fair that he should be struck down and lie useless. What good had it done him to believe in God? Bitterness welled in her and blinded her to the beauty at which she stared.

The clatter of Ellie's cleaning cart in the hall roused her, and she turned from the window and felt herself grow rigid as she saw Bill looking at her. She stared at him, unable to move. Then a slight grin quirked one corner of his mouth, and his lips parted.

"Mo-thr—"

The word came haltingly, with a slurring, dragging of the sound like a record that had run down.

"Bill!"

Her hands reached out as she crossed swiftly to the bed and took his one unbandaged hand in hers, unable to keep the tears from spilling over as she repeated his name over and over. She felt the slight answering pressure from the fingers of his hand as he looked up at her, a frown creasing his forehead under the line of the bandage. He tried to lift his one free hand and stared up at the bottle of intravenous solution. His mouth worked to shape words.

"Wher—am—I?"

"In the hospital, Bill. But you're going to be all right. I know it!"

"How—lo—" He could not finish the word and looked at her helplessly.

"Oh, it doesn't matter! The important thing is you're conscious. We've been waiting for this."

But he frowned as he stared up at her, trying to work out for himself what had happened.

"Were-ri-ding." The words came more slowly with the syllables slurring together unlike his normal speech pattern.

"Ina—caaar." He closed his eyes and then opened them slowly to focus on her face. "Thass—all-memb—"

He closed his eyes again, and Mrs. Andrews leaned over him.

"No, Bill," she said, her voice urgent. "Don't go to sleep. Stay here! Stay awake!" She put her hands on his shoulders as though to pull him back to her, and his eyelids slowly lifted and then closed again.

Mrs. Andrews reached to press the light for the nurse and hurried to the door. She looked out into the empty hall, seeing only Ellie's cart, and called, "Nurse!"

Ellie came to the door of the next room and Mrs. Andrews said, "Call the nurse, and get a doctor. Hurry! Bill woke up, but he's gone to sleep again. Hurry!"

She hovered anxiously in the doorway long enough to see Ellie drop the pile of dirty sheets she was holding and race along the hall and down the stairs. Then Mrs. Andrews hurried back to Bill and talked to him and patted his cheeks, her hands trembling. It could not be natural for him to go to sleep. He must be drifting back into unconsciousness. Why hadn't a nurse or the doctor been here to do something! Why hadn't she called them right away, instead of talking to Bill!

She moved aside as the nurse and doctor came in and, without a glance at her, pushed past to bend over Bill. The doctor listened to his heart and looked into his eyes while the nurse took his blood pressure and checked his pulse.

Finally the doctor straightened and looked across at her and smiled. "I think we've won this part of the battle."

"But why didn't he stay awake?"

"It's a very normal reaction. Not at all unusual in cases like this."

"It's not the same unconsciousness? He looks the way he did before."

The doctor shook his head. "It may seem like it to you, but there's a difference in his breathing. And there are other signs of improvement. He'll be awake naturally from now on."

She looked at him, frowning. "You said we've won this part of the battle. That means there's another?"

"Yes. Now comes regaining the use of his legs. There is still paralysis, though we won't know to what extent until we run further tests. Did he speak to you? Know you?"

She nodded, and he said, "Good. There's probably no mental impairment then, thankfully. But complete physical recovery? Well, don't give up hope, but don't expect too much, either."

She turned from him abruptly to keep him from seeing the determination that flushed her face and thinned her lips. That would be her part, helping Bill return to normal. She listened as the doctor went on explaining Bill's condition and the treatment he needed.

"Unfortunately, we don't have the best of facilities here for therapy. We're in a rather poor section, without resources to draw from. In fact, the only reason we have a hospital at all is because some rich man, years ago, passing through on his way South, got sick, and almost died because there was no hospital here. He just barely made it to Louisville alive. As a result, he gave money for this hospital and a stipulated yearly sum for maintenance. We're glad for it, of course. But we don't have enough money to get equipment to keep up with all the medical developments. Maybe we don't need it since we are so near Louisville. I'm on staff at a hospital there, but I spend the greater part of my time here."

He walked over to stare out the window and added almost to himself, "I grew up here and know what the people need. In a way, I think of them as my responsibility."

Mrs. Andrews was impatient with his personal feelings. There was so much she needed to know about Bill. She broke in on his thoughts. "What will he need that you can't give him?"

"Help in exercise. Massage. Personal attention. We don't have the staff to spare—"

"That's why *I'm* here," she interrupted. "Tell me what to do."

He turned to face her. "I just wanted you to know our limitations. When he can be moved, he can be flown other places. They're expensive, of course."

"Can he recover here as well?"

The doctor shook his head in warning. "You must understand, Mrs. Andrews, that I'm not saying positively at this point that he will recover. I think his chances are good, but I can't guarantee it."

"I understand that." It was an effort to keep the impatience from her voice. "But if he needs special treatment or special equipment, I'll arrange for it."

"Do you have another place in mind you want to take him?"

She shook her head. There was no need for him to know her business. No reason for him to know that she would have to go to Emily and Walter for help if Bill's expenses became too heavy. No need for anyone to know how difficult that would be. But she would do it if it would help Bill recover.

The doctor stood thinking, studying Bill's papers and charts. "I would suggest doing what we can here first to see what progress he makes. You could take him home, of course, after a while. It would be perfectly safe to fly him, naturally. But I would recommend keeping him here. Living where you do would confine him indoors during the months of ice and snow. Here the weather is milder, and if he makes the kind of recovery we are hoping for, he can be outside a good deal—in a wheelchair at least."

Mrs. Andrews listened as the doctor outlined a schedule for her to follow. It would be time-consuming, but it would be a relief to have something active to do instead of just sitting and watching Bill lie helpless.

The doctor started toward the door and then stopped and half turned to look at her. "You can't do this alone, you know," he warned. "His cooperation is essential. If he gets discouraged and wants to give up, it will make your job harder."

"He won't give up. He doesn't give up easily on anything."

Still the doctor hesitated in the doorway, gnawing at his lip as he looked back at her. "I must warn you also not to expect a miracle."

She straightened and looked at him across the narrow expanse of Bill's bed. Her voice crackled with anger as she answered, "I never expect miracles. I do not believe in miracles."

He looked back at her thoughtfully. "I have been in this business for a long time," he said finally. "Long enough to know that miracles do occur." He looked from her to Bill and back again. "This sounds harsh, I know. But I must say in all honesty that, if your son recovers fully, with no ill effects, you will have to acknowledge that it was a miracle."

He turned then and pushed through the door. Mrs. Andrews felt for the chair by the bed and sat down, anger sweeping her. Life never had been easy. If she had allowed it, it would have swept her under many times. And she had never counted on a miracle to help her. She would not give up now. She would see to it that Bill recovered. She and Bill, working together, would bring about this—this miracle.

She sat by the bed, holding his hand, watching him, thinking how excited Peggy would be at the news. Peggy, of course, would give God the credit. Well, let her, if it made her feel better.

Bill wakened again briefly in the late afternoon, and she was thankful she had stayed with him through the long day. He woke again in the evening, just before her usual time to leave. Each time, the doctor came immediately to examine him.

"Will he be all right through the night? Should I stay with him?"

"No, he isn't restless. He's sleeping quietly and naturally. The nurse will keep a close watch on him. But everything indicates that he is responding well and will be increasingly alert and wakeful. Get a good night's sleep yourself, so that you'll be able to help him tomorrow. He'll need your support and encouragement as he begins to understand his condition and his prospects."

The nurse came in to check on him, and Mrs. Andrews turned reluctantly and went downstairs and out the front door. As she stepped onto the porch, a slight figure detached itself from the shadows and joined her.

"I was workin' late. So I—I thought you'd not mind if I waited to walk you back to Grandma's." Ellie's voice was shy and uncertain sounding but deepened with warmth as she added, "I'm sure glad he's wakin' up."

Irritation swept Mrs. Andrews' tired frame at the admiration and interest coloring the girl's voice. She did not want to share Bill with anyone at this point, and certainly not with this girl! She did not even try to carry on a conversation with Ellie as they walked through the quiet streets and out to the small house beyond the edge of town. They stepped into the kitchen, and Mrs. Withrow looked up from the rocking chair by the window.

"Glad to hear the news. Been an anxious time for you."

"How did you know?" Surprise showed on her face.

"Ellie come home for supper. She said you hadn't eaten none, so I saved some for you."

Mrs. Andrews opened her mouth to protest and then realized she was ravenously hungry. Mrs. Withrow uncovered a kettle and ladled out a bowl of thick, steaming soup and set out a loaf of fresh-baked bread. Ellie said a shy goodnight as Mrs. Andrews sat down at the table. Mrs. Withrow poured them each a cup of hot tea and pulled the rocking chair nearer the table.

"He knew you, did he? When he come to?"

"Yes. But not where he was or what had happened."

"That'll come. Best not to have it all at once. How old is he?"

"Seventeen."

" 'Bout Ellie's age."

Mrs. Andrews ate silently. She did not want to know anything about the family. They were nothing to her. Finally, as the soup warmed and relaxed her, she knew she owed her hostess some show of interest. The habit of courtesy made her ask, "How long has she lived with you?"

"Since she was a little thing."

Mrs. Withrow rocked in silence, sipping her tea. "Her mother died when Ellie was wee. Her father—my son—

couldn't take care of her all alone, so she come to me."

"She's a pretty girl."

Mrs. Withrow nodded. "Her mother was pretty—and gentle. Too gentle. My son——" She stopped and rocked back and forth, the cup she held clicking against the saucer as her fingers trembled.

"My son was stubborn all his life, always sure he was right, sure he knew everythin' there was to know. Nobody could tell him nothin'. He grew up that way, and there was no changin' him. He fell in with a drinking crowd. Around here that's mighty easy to do. From then on, he changed, got mean. It got so folks was scared of him. 'Course it was worst on Martha. The times he come home drunk— not knowin' what he was doin'——" Her voice was brooding and her eyes sad as she looked off across the room.

"Then there wasn't no money for food and other things Martha needed, and she took sick. After Ellie was born— well, it took somethin' out of her. She wasn't strong any- way. Took cold easy. Then she took it hard when she knew Ellie wasn't quite right. She was such a pretty, dainty little thing. So things got worse. When Martha died, I took Ellie. Jim lived here when he wasn't off somewheres. That's his room you've got."

Mrs. Andrews wished the relentless story would stop. But she was sure there was more to the story, and she lis- tened as the tired voice went on.

"It was so useless. So useless for his life to be wasted. It didn't need to be. God knows how I prayed." She ges- tured helplessly with one hand. "He got himself mixed up in a fight when he was too drunk to know it was none of his business. There's too much feudin' goin' on. Not just here but all over. Maybe we see it more here, where we're off by ourselves some. That's the trouble with hate. It never does nobody good. It just takes away. Takes away a body's reason and good sense—and sometimes his life."

She reached to set her cup on the table. "So Ellie's all that's left to me. I'm aimin' to shield her all I can. There's a lot about life she don't understand, can't ever understand. There's a lot in life that'll hurt her. But she's got a special protection I give her every time she goes out. It's 'bout the only thing I can do for her now, at my age. I just ring her round with prayer and ask God to walk with her.

5

On the Road to Recovery

THE QUIET OF THE NIGHT intensified in her mind the memory of Mrs. Withrow's voice repeating itself as Mrs. Andrews lay sleepless, staring out at the star-studded sky through the small window under the sloping roof. Though she wanted to, she could not dismiss the story as just a tear-jerker, a plea for sympathy. The pain of the loss of her son was too real in Mrs. Withrow's face and voice. And yet, it was not just his loss she felt. It was the waste of his life. The thought flashed through her mind with certainty. She could sympathize, for she had faced the loss of Bill.

But there was another side to the story. The brutal drunk who was Mrs. Withrow's son only deserved what had happened to him. He had brought it on himself by his actions. But Bill did not deserve what had happened to him. And neither had John.

Her thoughts shied away from the painful thought of her husband and then were drawn back to memories of him—his gentleness, his patience, the determination he had shown when she had been angry about his coming with Bill for the summer. She remembered the simple, quiet way he had answered when she had turned on him with scornful words about his going to church.

"I've found what I should have had all my life, Elizabeth.

The children showed me the way, and I'm so grateful to them. Won't you join us?"

She remembered all too well the hard, angry words she had lashed back to him, declaring her independence of any help, especially from God.

The memories hurt and brought the tears she had refused to let come until now. She threw her arm over her face to stifle the sound from Ellie and from Mrs. Withrow, who had said, in spite of the tragedy her life had seen, "We know God's ways is best."

They aren't! I can't—I won't believe that. Not in this situation. Both John and Bill had so much to give. Now John is gone, and Bill lies crippled. I will not accept that kind of weak sentimentality. Someone has to assume the blame!

She finally dropped into a restless sleep and woke early, still tired. But the memory of Bill brought her out of bed eagerly to dress quickly and go downstairs to the smell of strong coffee and bacon.

"Mornin'." Mrs. Withrow turned from the stove with a plate which had been set to warm on the back of the stove. "Set down and eat before you go."

"Oh, no thank you. I'll get something at the hospital."

"From that cook?" Mrs. Withrow's voice summed up her contempt. "You've eaten her suppers. You don't want to start the day that way."

She flipped two light corn cakes onto the plate with browned curls of thick bacon and poured a cup of coffee.

"Ellie's already gone, and I've got to get to my neighbor whose baby's 'bout due, and she's got it in her mind she won't go to the hospital. Just rinse your dishes and close the door when you leave. You got the room here, and from what Ellie says you might be here quite a spell workin'

over your son. Might as well eat with us too. Won't cost
you no more."

"I certainly will not impose on you. I'll pay for what I
eat."

"I know you will. You're a proud woman. I seen that
right from the start. But when there's trouble, we don't talk
about payin' our way. There's nobody stands alone in this
world. Even those who think they can, come to the place
sooner or later where they've got to ask help from someone.
And, from what I've seen, most people git around to askin'
help from God soon as trouble hits 'em."

She threw a sweater around her shoulders and went out,
closing the door against the brisk chill of the morning air.
Mrs. Andrews watched her bent figure move along the path
beside the window and then cross the wide stretch of ground
that lay between her and her nearest neighbor. She turned
from the window and sat down to breakfast, grateful for
the food but resenting the sermon that seemed to accom-
pany everything Mrs. Withrow did.

The early morning fog was heavy in the valley as she
walked quickly along the still empty streets. Stray wisps
circled toward her as she turned up the winding road to
the hospital, not stopping to watch the sun light the sky or
listen to the birds talking to each other. Eagerness to see
Bill quickened her pace, and she was breathing rapidly as
she entered the hospital. Her nose told her she had been
wise to drink Mrs. Withrow's strong, fragrant coffee.

The clicking of her heels along the hall and up the stairs
carried her confidence to Bill's room. But she stopped at
the door, suddenly afraid to push it open, fearful that yesterday had been a temporary wakening and that today he
would be lying motionless and unreachable. Taking a deep
breath, she gave the door a quick push and looked at Bill

from the doorway. His eyes turned toward her and the characteristic smile spread to light his face.

"Been—waaa-ting."

He brought the word out triumphantly and smiled up at her as she approached. But a question was clear in the expression in his eyes. She watched his lips work to form words, instinctively knowing what he would ask and dreading the answer she must give.

"Whe-rr-'s Daa-ad?"

She sat down and tightened the grip she already had on his one free hand. She looked down at the blanket, away from his face, trying to steady her trembling lips. When she finally dared turn to face him directly, she knew she did not have to put an answer in words.

Tears stood in his eyes as he forced out, "Waas-he-hurrrt-b-baaad?"

She shook her head. "No, he went quickly, Bob said."

"Bob?"

She could not keep the inner bitterness from showing in her voice as she replied, "No. He wasn't hurt at all. Not a scratch. Only you—you and Dad."

He closed his eyes for a long moment, the fight to control his emotions showing in the tightened grip on her hand. Then he asked, "How l-lo—"

She waited, but though his mouth worked, he could not frame the word; and she guessed at what he wanted to know. "How long has it been?"

He nodded.

"Well, let's see." She thought back. "It happened about three weeks ago."

Then as he looked up at her, unasked questions in his eyes, she told him all she knew about the accident.

"Peggy and I were coming home from California on

Monday, but Bob's telegram came Sunday," she explained. "He just said there had been an accident and that you were injured. That was all we knew, and we flew back at once that afternoon. Your uncle came with us. He helped take care of arrangements for—" She stopped and put her head down on the bed, and Bill slowly moved his hand to put it comfortingly on her shoulder.

She sat up straight after a moment and went on. "It seemed best for me to stay here with you while Peggy and your uncle took—took Dad back home. Bob went then also."

"Peg—coll-ege?"

"Yes. There was nothing more she could do here, and I insisted that she go on with her plans. I'm afraid she wastes too much time thinking of us, because she has written almost every day, wondering about you. I've saved the letters for you to read. I'm going to call her this evening with the good news."

She felt the pressure of his hand on hers as he smiled back at her. Then he moved his hand slowly to indicate his body.

"How—b-aaad?"

Her voice came quickly, confidently. "Oh, now that you are conscious, your recovery will come rapidly."

His head moved slowly against the pillow, shutting off her eager, positive words. "Caan't m-ooove—legs. Why?"

She swallowed hard against the fear she was trying to cover with her rush of confident words. "Bill, I don't know how long it will take, but I'm sure with the right kind of treatment you will be all right again. This is only a temporary paralysis. The doctor says therapy will help you. You will walk again!"

The words came out sounding brisk and sure, but inside she meant them as defiance of God. She would not *let* Bill be a permanent cripple, no matter what God's plans were.

When the doctor came in a little later, Bill asked the question again. They both watched intently as the doctor probed and tested and checked Bill's reflexes. He sat down beside the bed when he had finished and explained in detail all that had happened in Bill's body as a result of the accident.

"But I am increasingly hopeful that the paralysis is temporary. How rapidly you progress in restoring these muscles depends on you and how faithfully you do the exercises. No one else can help with them. Except to give encouragement."

He glanced at Mrs. Andrews' determined face and then back at Bill. "But don't push," he cautioned. "Work at them to the point where they tire you and it requires some effort to do them. But don't push yourself to the point of exhaustion."

Bill's mouth worked as he looked up at the doctor. "Plan to beee hoome Chrisss-mas."

"You've set yourself quite a goal." The doctor looked down at him, a frown wrinkling across his forehead. Then his face cleared, and he reached to put a firm grip on Bill's shoulder. "I'll not discourage you. You do your part, and we'll do ours, and maybe—just maybe—you'll get the results you're working for sooner than we expect.

Bill avidly read the typed instructions for exercises which he could do lying in bed and began them immediately. Gradually the doctor added others, and Bill followed the directions explicitly. While he exercised physically, he

talked, carefully measuring his words and learning to enun-
ciate slowly and clearly.

"Got—to—talk—right, Motherrr," he answered her urging to relax and not try so hard. "I'm gooo-ing—too—
preeech. Have too—be goood—speaker."

Mrs. Andrews bent quickly to retuck the sheet which
had come loose at the foot of the bed, to keep Bill from
seeing her face. She was sure it clearly showed the thought
that whirled through her mind. Not a preacher! No! She
would not let Bill waste himself that way.

But with it came the whisper, *Anything is better than to
have him lie a helpless cripple.* She argued back fiercely
but silently, *The God he believes in and wants to preach
about should have kept him from injury.*

She straightened then and said as calmly as possible,
"The next time the doctor comes, ask him to give you exercises for speech correction. I'm sure there is therapy they
give schoolchildren who have an impediment or other
speech difficulties."

The weeks passed slowly, with Mrs. Andrews' waking
hours bounded by the hospital walls and her sleeping hours
spent in the little room over Mrs. Withrow's kitchen. The
fall weather was so much warmer and sunnier than they
were used to at home that she was glad she decided to keep
Bill there to recuperate. The doctor encouraged her to get
Bill out of his wheelchair and to walk him back and forth
along the driveway, the brace he had been fitted with giving needed support.

The changing color of leaves was spectacular, and they
enjoyed the beauty as they walked and sat out each day
in the warm afternoon sun. As Mrs. Andrews knitted, Bill
talked, saying words over and over again. He got a dic-
tionary and went down column after column, repeating

words until they came clearly. And he memorized Scripture.

"It's a great time for it, Mother," he answered, when she urged him to let her get him other books. "It's OK to get me other books. But I've got to know the Bible when I start preaching, and I may never have a better chance to memorize. When I get back to school next semester, I'll have to catch up on so much work I won't have time to sit around like this."

He reached to the stack of books beside his wheelchair and picked up his Bible. "Test me on this one, will you, please? Ellie helped me with it this morning, early, before you came. She's learning verses, too."

He flipped the Bible to Psalm 100 and handed it to her. Then he leaned back in his chair and looked up at the blue sky through the green and gold leaves of the tree they were sitting under while he said the words.

> "Make a joyful noise unto the LORD, all ye lands.
> Serve the LORD with gladness: come before his
>   presence with singing.
>
> "Know ye that the LORD he is God:
> It is he that hath made us, and not we ourselves;
> We are his people, and the sheep of his pasture.
>
> "Enter into his gates with thanksgiving, and into
>   his courts with praise:
> Be thankful unto him, and bless his name.
>
> "For the LORD is good; his mercy is everlasting;
> And his truth endureth to all generations."

Mrs. Andrews held the Bible, but she did not look at it, would not look at it. In the silence between them, squirrels rustled leaves as they scampered in search of nuts and acorns. In the distance, someone was sawing down a tree, the sound a faint rasping back and forth that by contrast accentuated the peacefulness of their surroundings.

"Beautiful here, isn't it?" Bill said finally. "Quiet. Peaceful. I'm glad we're staying here. Seems like nothing could go wrong in the world if it were all like this."

"There's a great deal here that's wrong under the surface beauty and peace," Mrs. Andrews replied, remembering Mrs. Withrow's story.

"Yeah, I know. Ellie has told me a little about how things are here. It just proves that when people don't know God and don't want to know Him, there's bound to be trouble."

"Apparently trouble comes to those who claim to know Him, too. You are proof of that. And your father." She had not realized how savagely bitter her words were until she heard them echoing between them in the stillness and saw the troubled look on Bill's face. "Well, it's true," she insisted defiantly.

After a moment he said slowly, "I'm glad I'm going to get over this. But I could stand it if I didn't. The thing that bothered me most when I realized how badly I was hurt and knew what had happened to Dad was having you upset and bitter over it. I was afraid you would blame God. I know you don't think of Him the way I do, the way Peggy does. We wish you did!"

She looked down at the knitting in her lap, hearing the longing in his voice but unmoved by it.

After a few moments when she made no response, Bill said, " 'Know ye that the LORD he is God: it is he that hath made us . . . we are his people and the sheep of his pasture.' That's true, too, Mother."

She picked up her knitting without answering, the needles flashing in the sun as she worked quickly.

Bill watched her. "You know, knitting would exercise my fingers, wouldn't it? Is it hard to do?"

"It depends on what you make. A simple stitch is easy to learn. You wouldn't have to actually make something if all you want to do is to exercise your fingers. You could just knit a long straight piece and then unravel it and start over again. I'll get you a ball of cheap gray yarn to practice on, if you are really serious."

He was silent, watching her. Then he said, "Not gray, Mother. Get me however much yarn it would take to make a scarf. Get a shade of blue like—" He looked around and then up at the sky. "Get me some about that shade if you can find it."

Mrs. Andrews squinted at the deep blue above them. "It will be a little difficult to take a sample of that along to the store," she said drily. "But I'll get as near that shade as I can. A scarf of that color would look very pretty on Peggy."

They both looked around as Ellie crossed the grass toward them, her face bright with her shy smile, and handed Bill a letter.

"It just came. I got it when I went to see if Grandma had got her catalog."

"Thanks, Ellie." He looked at the envelope. "Good— from Peggy. It's about time she wrote." He tore open the envelope and then looked up at Ellie as she turned to leave. "Sit down and listen, if you have time," he invited. "Peggy's a good letter writer."

Ellie dropped down on the grass near Bill's chair, not seeing Mrs. Andrew's disapproving glance at him.

DEAR BOTH OF YOU,

Yes, I *know* I haven't written for two weeks. And I'm sorry, but life is *hectic!*

Bill, at this minute I'd give *anything* to be sitting in your wheelchair with absolutely no worries about term papers, exams, a speech final, copy due for the school paper, and a sketch I promised to help Sarah Elizabeth do for her design class.

OK—I don't really mean it of course—and I'm sure you'd trade with me in a minute. But life at college *is* busy, as you'll find out.

I'm so excited about how well you're doing! Bet you could make the wrestling team, with all that muscle buildup.

I envy your being able to memorize all that Scripture. I'm trying to memorize one verse a day, which is pretty skimpy compared to what you are doing.

Mother, Mrs. Withrow sounds great from what you have written about her. I'd like to sample some of her cooking. The food here is OK, but you'll notice I haven't raved about it. I'm *so* glad you found such a good place to stay, because I was so worried about it when I left (almost two months ago already!), not that I didn't think God would work it out, but I was worried because I just went off and left you without doing anything to help. (Wow, what a mixed sentence!)

Anyway—have you been to church at all? Could you go, Bill? Is it hard to get around in your wheelchair? Just be careful not to get at the top end of one of those hilly roads unless you've got good brakes on the chair!

Sarah Elizabeth and I are going to a really terrific church about a mile from campus. We're the only ones on our floor who go regularly, as far as we know. A couple of girls are interested in having a weekly Bible study, so we'll see what happens.

Bill, I've been going to ask you and keep forgetting, how many letters have you had from Candy?

Wish I could see you at Thanksgiving, but there's not enough time. What about Christmas? What shall we plan? Shall I come there? You won't be home by then, I don't suppose. Is it still warm there?

Aunt Emily calls me every Sunday night. She would really love to hear from you, Mother.

Please write, Bill! It's good exercise, you know, for both your fingers and your brain!

Say hi to Ellie for me.

Love,

PEGGY

"She sounds so nice," Ellie said softly, when Bill had finished and handed the letter to his mother to reread for herself. Then with a hesitant look at Mrs. Andrews, she said, "If you want to go to church sometime, Grandma and me'd be glad to take you to ours. I would of asked you before but Grandma said to wait a spell till you all were better and said you wanted to come. It's awful small, but the folks is right friendly."

Before Mrs. Andrews could refuse, Bill replied, "I would like! How about it, Mother?"

Her answer came reluctantly. "Well—I suppose. Perhaps we could try it once, when you are stronger."

She tried not to sound too ungracious in the face of Bill's eagerness. But it was too bad for Ellie to interfere. She glanced down at the girl as she knelt on the grass beside Bill's chair, looking up at him. When she saw the expression on Ellie's face, Mrs. Andrews looked sharply at Bill. He was laughing down at Ellie as he told a funny story about something that had happened to Peggy.

She was sure he was totally unaware of what Ellie's face revealed as her blue eyes fastened on him in rapt attention and her lips parted in a smile which bubbled into a laugh when he finished. The sun glinted on her shining blond head and sparkled the wisps of hair curling damply around her face in the warmth of the day. She was a pretty girl if one did not know that there was a lack in her which was not visible on the surface.

Mrs. Andrews tightened her lips as she watched them, her fingers momentarily stilled on her knitting. She would have to be alert—warn Bill if necessary. He was simply too nice to everyone, without making a distinction between people. That was all right if it was not carried too far. But Bill was too kindhearted for his own good. Without intending to, he could give Ellie the idea that he was interested in her.

She stood up abruptly. "Bill, you've sat long enough. It's time for more exercise. Ellie, I'm sure you have duties inside."

Ellie scrambled to her feet, ducking her head. "Yes'm." She stood poised for flight and looked down at Bill. "When you want, I'll show you our church."

"We'll do it real soon."

After she had left, skimming lightly across the grass, he looked up at his mother.

"I must admit that's one of the things I wonder about." He gestured after Ellie. "There she is, with no way of getting out of this life. And then there's Peggy, with all her opportunities. If anything about life doesn't seem fair, this is it."

"Yes, but remember, Peggy has worked hard for what she has. She's used her opportunities more than some would. And she has natural ability." She stopped, glancing briefly at Bill. Then, keeping her voice casual, she said, "You must remember that Ellie is not—well, not quite normal. She's very pretty—and sweet. But she isn't capable of the kind of life Peggy has. She *is* a little slow, you know, Bill."

She worked to keep the insistence from her voice, not wanting to sound too strong a warning if there was no need for it.

In the silence Bill sat looking off across the hillside which was alive with color. Then he smiled up at his mother. "I know. But someday she won't be. In heaven everyone is perfect."

6

A Misunderstanding Resolved

BILL'S VOICE echoed in Mrs. Andrews' ears as the days slipped by. The words, so simply spoken, were typical of his concern for someone else. It was a concern she had to admit she did not have.

By November, winter had begun to creep through the hills, and she felt the cold most in the early morning. She dressed quickly in the chill of her unheated room and hurried down to the warmth of the kitchen. She had come to look forward each day to the breakfast Mrs. Withrow had ready, and even to the few minutes of conversation at the table.

Sometimes Mrs. Withrow's comments and questions were too personal, and Mrs. Andrews was constantly on guard against revealing too much of herself. But her first impression that her landlady was simply a nosey busybody had shifted. Mrs. Withrow had a sincere interest in people and had seen enough, even in her limited circumstances in this little town, to have a sharp insight into human nature. Even the one-sentence sermons did not irritate as much as they had at first, for they were evidence that her faith in God was the core of her life. Mrs. Andrews sensed that it was only Mrs. Withrow's faith that had made her life endurable.

But the old lady was a direct person and did not waste words when there was something she wanted to say.

Mrs. Andrews came down earlier than usual one morning, just as Ellie was finishing her breakfast. She mumbled a confused, "Morning," in response to Mrs. Andrews' greeting and jumped up from the table, grabbing a heavy sweater from the back of her chair.

She slipped quickly out the door, buttoning the sweater as she went. Mrs. Andrews carried Ellie's dishes to the sink as she said, "She's in a hurry to get to work."

"It ain't that. She just don't feel easy around you."

Mrs. Andrews turned, still holding the dishes, to see Mrs. Withrow looking at her, the expression in her eyes both sad and accusing.

"I'm sorry." But the words sounded stiff and cold even to her ears. "I certainly have no intention of hurting the child. If I've said or done anything to offend her, I assure you, it was unintentional."

Mrs. Withrow served the warm plate of food and poured coffee for each of them and sat down, stirring hers in silence. Finally she said slowly, "Ellie's not good at words. She's not bright in book ideas. But she's good in feelings. There's some things a body knows without it bein' put in words. One is knowin' when someone likes you—or when someone *don't* like you, don't want you around. That's somethin' doesn't have to be said. When you know someone feels that way about you, you can't act natural. You get all shut in, start doin' things wrong. When that happens, it make you seem dumber than you are."

She looked across the table, her face and voice stern. "I ain't goin' to let that child be hurt. Not by nobody. Whether it's on purpose or purely by accident."

"I haven't found that life spares anyone from hurts," Mrs. Andrews began defensively.

Mrs. Withrow nodded agreement. "But there's some can

take it better than others. Ellie—she don't have the toughness needed for some kind of hurts." She got up stiffly to rinse her cup at the sink.

Mrs. Andrews sat creasing and uncreasing the paper napkin in her fingers. Her natural reserve and the years of loneliness bottled up inside struggled with the urgent feeling that she wanted to share herself with this equally proud and lonely woman. There was a bond between them that she was more conscious of after every conversation.

"We are each one thinking of the best interests of our own child," she said finally.

Mrs. Withrow came to stand across the table from her. "You're lookin' out for your son, and I'm thinkin' of my Ellie.

Mrs. Andrews nodded. "Bill is—" She stopped, searching for words to describe him.

"I ain't even seen him. Don't know him 'cept from what I hear, and that's mostly from Ellie. It's all good."

"He is friendly—kind. He sees everyone alike. He might not realize that his kindness could be taken as—" She struggled for the right words to make her meaning clear without offending. "He might not realize that it could be interpreted as more than kindness."

"You're sayin' the kindness could never be love."

"No! He's only seventeen."

"Her paw was married at that age."

"Yes, but Bill has to finish high school. Then he plans on college and probably school after that. When he is well and we leave here, this experience will all be in the past. He will, of course, remember his time here; but it will be only a memory."

She looked up at Mrs. Withrow's brown, lined face as she went on explaining. "He likes Ellie because he is a person who likes everyone. He always has. There is hardly anyone he can't get along with. He likes Ellie the way he likes everyone," she repeated firmly.

"That's all?"

"Yes." Then, in the silence, without thinking, she added, "And because he feels sorry for her."

Mrs. Withrow turned sharply. "He can keep his sorriness!" She flung her shawl around her shoulders and took a basket on her arm. "Shut the door when you leave," she ordered and stalked out.

Mrs. Andrews went to the window and looked after her as she moved along the path and took the road toward town. In spite of the bent shoulders which thrust her head forward in such a painful looking position, pride and dignity walked with her. Mrs. Andrews felt the renewed stirring that they were alike in spirit in many ways. Mrs. Withrow was rightly on guard to protect a shy, adoring girl from hurt. And she—she had to guard Bill from the kindness and sympathy of his nature.

Instead of going directly to Bill's room when she arrived at the hospital, she went to the desk and asked to speak to the doctor.

"He should be in his office. Just go along and knock," the nurse said cheerfully. "If he's there, you can see him. If not, he'll be there soon."

The doctor's voice answered her knock, and she entered the office and took the chair he indicated.

She plunged in immediately. "When will Bill be completely recovered?"

"Now wait a minute!" He held up a hand in protest. "He's made tremendous progress, but we're not to the point of talking about complete recovery. Not to take up his regular life. Not yet."

"When, then?"

He was serious as he looked back at her determined face. "Is there some problem? You're not satisfied with his progress? With the treatment?"

"Yes, of course." She took a deep breath and forced herself to relax. "But I would like to begin to make plans. I have a home and other responsibilities. We have been here now almost three months. If I had some idea how much longer it will be until it is wise to move him home, it would help me plan. I'm remembering that you said weeks back that he could be flown home even then. But we agreed that the wisdom of doing it was the main factor to consider."

"If you are talking about putting him back into his normal life, I would say two months at the earliest. Could be even four or five."

Her mind figured quickly. This was past the middle of November. Two months would take it into January. Five would be April. That would be too long to remain here. She rose. "Two months, then."

"Just a minute." The doctor stood up too. "Let me tell you why I don't recommend rushing him home too fast. Taking him back into the pressures of his former circumstances, to a faster way of life than we have here, to seeing his friends with their normal life, could give him a psychological setback, even if he could swing it physically."

She looked back at him over her shoulder. "Do you think I would do anything to hurt his chance of recovering? But we do need a goal, and you've given it to us. Two months."

Bill was enthusiastic when she told him, even though she warned him of the doctor's doubt.

"That means, if we push it up just a couple of weeks, I can get back into school the second semester. If I take a couple of extra subjects and go to summer school, I can get into college next fall, after all! I'd better get busy on an application."

His enthusiasm was contagious and lifted Mrs. Andrews' spirits. It even made her able to hide her reluctance about attending church, since Bill was so eager to go. Anything that would help him was important. She agreed they would go with Ellie and Mrs. Withrow the Sunday before Thanksgiving.

Though her experiences in any kind of church had been limited, she was totally unprepared for the informality of the service in the little frame building. There was no choir and little order of any kind to the service. The man who presided asked for song choices, and Mrs. Andrews could not understand how he culled out a recognizable number from the responses that were shouted. When he asked for prayer needs, some stood with brief words, others with long, rambling requests. During the prayer that followed, there were frequent exclamations from others in the congregation, who interrupted with their own prayers voiced out loud.

She had no idea what the preacher said in his sermon, busy as she was in wrapping her reserve around her as a guard against the frank curiosity of the people. She supposed Bill would call their curiosity friendliness. Now and then, even in the middle of the sermon, those around leaned over to shake hands first with her and then with Bill, assuring them they were welcome in the church.

Bill was enjoying himself, apparently completely at home in this type of service, not at all disturbed by its informality nor by the curious questions he was asked when the service was over. Ellie hovered nearby but kept close to her grandmother and avoided Mrs. Andrews.

When Mrs. Withrow stopped beside his wheelchair, Bill
looked up at her, his grin spreading to light his eyes. "It's
sure nice to meet you after hearing all about you from
Ellie."

Her eyes studied him. "I shoulda been up to see you
afore this. Feel like I know you from Ellie's talk."

"She's sure been a help to me. Those first days when I
couldn't do anything, Ellie came in on her time off and just
sat there and was a friend."

Mrs. Withrow looked down at him her eyes watchful.

Bill smiled over at Ellie as he went on. "I guess the thing
that made it easiest for us to get acquainted is that, when I
asked her to read me something—that was when I first
came to—she read me the Twenty-third Psalm."

Mrs. Andrews heard the sharp intake of Mrs. Withrow's
breath as she took a quick step forward, her face darkening.
Before she could say anything, Bill went on easily, "Of
course, then I found out she wasn't reading it. She knew it
by heart. Since then we've been learning other verses. I
say them first, and then she does, and we sort of help each
other."

Mrs. Withrow turned abruptly without a word and
walked off down the road, with Ellie trailing after her. Bill
watched them go, a worried frown on his forehead.

"Boy, I sure goofed about something. I wonder what
sent her off like that? Doesn't she want Ellie to learn Bible
verses?"

"She is a very unpredictable person. And very protective
where Ellie is concerned."

Mrs. Andrews maneuvered the wheelchair along the
road and through the streets of the town, debating how
much more she should say. Finally she said, "Bill, don't

let Ellie get too dependent on your friendship, because it will be very difficult for her when we leave."

He nodded soberly. "I've thought of that. But she doesn't have close friends her own age here. She's such a nice kid. I wish Peggy were here to talk to her."

"You do get letters from Candy?"

"Well, yeah—but what's that got to do with Ellie?"

"I thought—if Ellie knew—if she realized you had a girl—"

"Mom, Candy and I are just friends!"

She argued back stubbornly. "I still think it would be easier if Ellie knew you had friends back home—a girl you liked. You can see how, in a situation like this, she could dream of something that is impossible. When she has so little as it is, you don't want to be the one to hurt her more, unintentionally."

"We're friends, Mom. We understand each other," Bill answered.

Walking home that evening, Mrs. Andrews wondered what to expect from her hostess. When she opened the door to the kitchen, Mrs. Withrow was sitting at the table, her hands folded in front of her on the plastic tablecloth.

She looked across the room. "Set down, will you?"

When Mrs. Andrews faced her across the table, she stared down at her clenched hands. Her voice was low as she said, "I've got to tell you that I'm sorry. I've been keepin' mean thoughts about you lately. And about your son. I see now that I was wrong. I don't have to fear that he'll do anything hurtful to Ellie. Oh, I know the way she thinks of him she's goin' to be hurt. But not on purpose by him. She's got a heart that's longin' for love and tenderness, and he won't ever be the one to give it. So it'll be hard on her."

Mrs. Andrews reached out. "I don't understand—"

A look of pain was in Mrs. Withrow's eyes as she answered, "Don't you see? He never once let on he knew
she couldn't read! He made it seem like she was just as
bright as anyone. Better even, because she didn't have to
read them verses. Because she knew them by heart. He
acted as though it was just natural. You've got a fine boy,
and I'm sorry I had some doubtful thoughts about him.
It's because he's a believer, ain't it?"

"I—I don't know. I—suppose so."

She sat looking at the other woman, thinking how little
it took sometimes to turn a person's opinion. But Bill's attitude was not because he was a believer, as Mrs. Withrow
so quaintly said, but because it was his natural characteristic to be kind.

Just like his father. The thought was so strong it was
like words spoken out loud.

Through the hurt of the memories that came, she heard
Mrs. Withrow say, "I'd be proud if you and your son would
eat the Thanksgiving meal with us. Ellie and me, we feel
the lonesomeness most at holiday times. Like most folks
do, I guess."

Mrs. Andrews looked away from her. She and Bill were
alone, too, and needed empty places filled. She heard herself say, in a formal acceptance, "We would like that very
much. Bill will especially appreciate your good cooking.
But can't I—"

She stopped herself just in time. This proud old lady
would not want help if it implied she could not do it herself. So she said instead, "I haven't cooked for so long,
I'm going to forget how. Couldn't we work together on the
dinner?"

"I'd like that right well."

Thanksgiving morning was clear and sunny but cold. Mrs. Andrews stopped on the hospital porch to tuck an extra blanket around Bill before bringing him down the road past the closed shops. They were stopped half a dozen times along the way by people who had seen them in church and who leaned over the fence or stopped on the road to chat. Most of them were older people, and she commented on that to Bill as they went along.

He nodded. "This town is a lot like the one we were in this summer." He looked around as he spoke. "That one was sort of shut off by the hills, too. Made you think you were in another world. In some ways it was nice, and in some ways not so good. I guess most of the kids in these places go to the city for work and never come back here to live." He took a deep breath. "I like it here, though. No one rushes around in a hurry to get somewhere. And if you don't get something done today, there's always to-morrow."

"So I've noticed," Mrs. Andrews retorted. "I went into the store that time to buy the yarn for you and thought I'd still be waiting for it at Christmas. They move so slowly, at least in that store—as though time didn't have any meaning. I must say, I didn't find them overly friendly."

He laughed around at her. "You scared them off, Mom. You are so very definitely from another world. You always give the impression of being so self-assured and—and crisp."

"Bill! That makes me sound very unpleasant!"

"I didn't mean it that way. But you know you could never live here permanently. You're too energetic. You'd wear everyone out. You'd want things done *now*, today, instead of when it's convenient."

"Nonsense! Oh, I'll admit I don't want to stay here a

moment longer than necessary. But as to being energetic, there's no one more so than Mrs. Withrow."

"I still say it's a different kind of life. A different way of being busy."

Mrs. Andrews stopped the wheelchair as they reached Mrs. Withrow's house and turned to look around her. The town itself was only a few hundred yards behind them, but it could have been miles away as they stood in the silence of the day. A rising wind rustled through the leaves that were still clinging to the branches. Two squirrels leaped from a tree branch to the roof of the house built against the shelter of the hill. It all blended into a way of life so different from anything she had known.

The thought that came involuntarily shocked her. *How easy my life has been*.

But she argued back silently, *It hasn't been easy*. There was the bitterness that had existed through the years between herself and Emily, the family antagonism when she had married John, the early years of poverty and struggle, the heartbreak of sending Jane to live with Emily and Walter, the lack of understanding between herself and John, her objection to his faith in God and the children's, and now his loss—

She thrust it all away in the swift motion she made to back the wheelchair up the one low porch step.

Bill protested, "Mom, get Ellie to help."

"Nonsense. Any woman who has ever pushed a baby buggy or a stroller can do this alone. These big wheels make the chair move easily."

Ellie stood framed in the doorway, a shy, welcoming smile curving her lips as she held the door wide.

"Boy, does that smell good!" Bill sniffed a deep breath and sighed in anticipation. "Bet I can guess what it is.

Turkey, dressing—" He took another deep breath. "Pumpkin pie?"

Ellie shook her head. "Apple pie. But it's pumpkin bread. Grandma makes it best of anyone in these parts."

"In the whole world, from the smell of it," Bill exclaimed. He looked around the kitchen and at the table along one wall, set for the meal. "Put me someplace out of the way, but not too far from the table." He grinned at Ellie's happy face as she pushed his chair over to where he would sit.

Mrs. Withrow straightened from leaning to baste the turkey. "It'll only be a piece till the bird's done. Your Ma's got a fancy salad she's bound to make, so we'd best give her room."

When dinner was ready and they were seated at the table, Mrs. Withrow looked at Bill. "I s'pose you're the man here today. But I've been askin' the blessing as long as I can remember, so I reckon I'll go on doin' it. Maybe you'll want to say one, too, when I git through. I guess you figure you've got a lot to be thankful for along with a lot that ain't so good. But that's the way life is—we have to take the bad with the good and thank the Lord for all the good He does send."

She stopped for a moment and then went on. "One thing more I want to say. I've found that words alone don't make a prayer. If it don't come from the inside, it ain't a prayer no matter how fancy the words might be. And today I'm thankful for new friends. Didn't think I would be when I first saw you. Proves you can't tell about people from what you see of 'em on the outside. But you two are some of the good the Lord sent us this year, and I'm mighty glad for you."

Bill reached out a hand toward his mother. "I've been wanting to say something, too, for a long time. Maybe to-

day is the best time, since it's Thanksgiving Day." He
stopped and gripped his hands together on the table in
front of him. His voice was husky as he went on without
looking around at them. "This is going to be hard to say
and hard to listen to and—and I may have trouble getting
it all out. But—we're both small families, and we're both
missing part of the family. I'm missing Dad—very much—"
His voice cracked, and he stopped.

Then he steadied it and went on. "But then I remember
that he's with God, in heaven. The Bible says that's a wonderful place to be, better than here. So I'm glad Dad's
there. I can't wish him back here, even though I miss him
so much. We had such a great time this summer. But I
just—I just want all the rest of the family—all of us—to be
sure we'll be with him in heaven someday."

Mrs. Andrews did not look at Bill as he talked, could
not look at him. She was grateful this time for Mrs. Withrow's lengthy prayer, which gave her time to recover. She
was shaken by the plea in Bill's voice that she could not re-
spond to. She would be outwardly happy for Bill's sake.
But the growing understanding of what she had lost she
would have to endure in private. Perhaps some day she
would have to decide whether she would cross the bridge of
accepting what John and the children had, but not yet. She
was not ready to decide that yet. God was still someone to
oppose, not to love.

7

Old Man Jenkins

PEGGY'S LETTER the following week was full of exclamations about her visit with her roommate for Thanksgiving. But it was bursting with questions as well.

What *are* we doing about Christmas? Aunt Emily keeps talking about all of us being together, but I don't see how we can when we're all so scattered. I *think* she means we should all be with them, but I don't like to think of Christmas in California—maybe it's 'cause I was there once and the memory is sort of—I don't know, kind of unpleasant.

Is there *any* chance you two will be home? I mean to our house? If so, they could fly there, which I think they'd be willing to do, especially if it were best for Bill. But if you have to stay there, I'll come too. I don't suppose there's any chance of putting Uncle Walter and Aunt Emily and Jane up there, maybe?

Anyway, whatever we do for Christmas, I'm through here the Friday before, and I get two weeks off. The super thing is that there are kids from school who are driving almost to that town, and I can ride with them. It's someone Sarah Elizabeth knows, and they're great kids, so you don't have to worry about careless drivers or anything like that. I don't suppose you'll have any snow for Christmas there, will you? Or not much anyway—not like at home, which I will kind of miss.

But the really, *really* super thing is that if we have to be down there instead of at home, Dan said he would leave home a couple of days early and detour around to take me back to school, which is quite a detour since it'll take him a long way out of his way. But he wants to see Bill (and me too, I hope!) which is why he offered.

Soooo—let me know what you decide.

Sorry I've rattled on without saying how wonderful it is to hear how well things are going there. Thanks for all two letters, Bill! I'm sure curious to know what you're so busy doing that you don't write as often as you did.

It is *cold* here. Got to run. Got two *long* papers due Friday.

WRITE!

Love from me.

Mrs. Andrews folded the letter carefully and put it back in the neatly opened envelope. To have Emily and Walter with them for Christmas *anywhere* was out of the question. There was too much upsetting her as it was, and the added strain of being with them was more than she could take.

But when Bill read the letter, he was full of excited plans and questions. "What do you think, Mom? Suppose we could find them a place? I'd sure like to meet them, since Peggy has talked so much about them, and Uncle Walter took time to come back with you."

Mrs. Andrews shook her head. "No! It's out of the question, Bill. It may be possible for them to come for a visit after we go home, or next summer. Perhaps we could consider something for next Christmas. But not now, not here."

"Yeah, I guess it wouldn't work." He brightened. "But

anyway, Peggy will be here. And it'll be neat having Dan. I'm glad he and Peggy are still dating."

"If they are, it's only by letter." Her voice was sharp and critical, and Bill looked across at her.

"He's really a terrific guy, Mom. When you get to know him."

"I know him well enough." The tone of her voice closed off further discussion.

But Bill ignored the finality in her voice and argued, "If he's coming down, we'll want him to know he's welcome. We don't want him to feel in the way."

"I have no intention of being rude or impolite, Bill. I hope you know me well enough to remember that I am never deliberately impolite to people, even those I don't especially care for."

"But sometimes the politeness is only in the words." Bill looked at her anxiously, groping for the words to express himself. "If the *feeling* isn't there, the words don't mean much. Like Ellie—" He stopped and looked away from the indignant expression on his mother's face.

"What about her?"

"Well—she thinks you don't like her."

"I certainly don't dislike her. I must say I don't think about her one way or another. She's not that important to me."

"That's what I'm saying, I guess, Mother," Bill went on slowly, his voice reaching for words. "You make a difference in the value of people. Like Ellie not being important because she's a little bit slow in thinking. And Dan because his parents were once refugees. Even though that's a long time ago now, you still remember it when the rest of us have forgotten. It still matters to you."

Bill's voice and eyes were troubled as he looked across

the expanse of the bed and then stretched his hand out in appeal. "No one is better than anyone else, Mom. If God doesn't think so, neither should we."

"Very well, Bill. You've said what you think. Now, let's close the subject, please."

She took a notebook from her bag, looking away from the plea for understanding that was so plain in his eyes. "We must make some plans for Christmas. I think I can arrange for Peggy to stay at Mrs. Withrow's. Ellie has offered to share her room, since mine has only a single bed. When we know how long Dan will be here, I'll make inquiries for a place for him to stay, probably at the motel. Now, I've been thinking of Christmas gifts. I've seen several things in the store here that Peggy might need and like. But I may have to take that morning bus to Louisville and spend a day shopping."

She kept her voice brisk and businesslike to cover the deep hurt Bill's words had caused. Life was just not as simple as he seemed to picture it. Dan as a person was not good enough for Peggy; it had nothing whatever to do with his background and family. As for Ellie, she was sweet, yes. But she was an uneducated small-town girl who had crossed their paths only incidentally. But there was no point in going into all that with Bill. He would not understand that sometimes one *had* to make a difference in people.

For now her main problem was to survive the remaining weeks here and get herself and Bill back to their normal life. The immediate need was to write Emily and Walter explaining the impossibility of their all getting together for Christmas. It would be a hard letter to write, and she rehearsed careful phrases in her mind.

Backward area—no place for all to be together—difficult

time of year to travel—roads could be treacherous, as you know from being here, Walter—perhaps when Bill is well and we are back home we can make plans. She deliberately left the future unformed and indefinite.

As she walked back to the hospital from the post office, her mood was as somber as the day, which was overcast with heavy clouds. An indefinable sense of things being out of joint weighed on her. *And,* she thought, *there really is no reason to feel so depressed.*

Peggy was obviously happy at school, enjoying every part of college life and having no financial worries. Bill was improving rapidly. She could not even feel sorry for John, if what Bill had said was true—that he was in heaven, with God, happy. If one could believe all that.

That left herself. And she was not happy. The admission came all by itself. She had not ever really been happy in all of her life. She stopped on the hospital steps and turned to look over the countryside. The leaves were almost entirely gone from the trees and lay brown and sodden along the ground, which was still wet from last night's cold rain. Mist rose slowly from the low places in the valley, shrouding bushes and giving a ghostlike quality to the atmosphere. The beauty and sparkle of the past weeks, that had lifted her spirits in spite of her anxiety about Bill, were gone as completely as the sun. Winter had come to the hills to match the winter of her spirits.

She had built a wall around herself to shut God out and deny Him any right to her life. But perhaps—it was a desolating thought—perhaps she had only succeeded in shutting herself off from life and love and real happiness.

She turned, then, and slowly lifted one foot at a time up each step to the hospital entrance. In spite of Bill's progress, it was hard to face the daily routine of exercises. It re-

quired effort each day to get him from the wheelchair to
the crutches which he used to walk repeatedly back and
forth down the long hall. She was grateful for his determination. If she had had to have courage for him as well
as for herself, she would have been discouraged. But even
so, the weeks had been long, and she was suddenly aware
of how tired she was.

She opened the door to Bill's room and stopped. He was
sitting in his wheelchair with Ellie kneeling beside him,
both absorbed in something he was holding. Bill looked
up as she came toward them, a smile lighting his face.

"Look! Won't these make super gifts? Someone Ellie
knows makes them."

Mrs. Andrews looked at the carved wooden objects
Bill was holding. One was a salad bowl, a curved wooden
spoon forming the rim. Another was a basket with a bunch
of grapes hidden among intertwined leaves forming the han-
dle. Two squirrels sat together nibbling on nuts. A fourth
carving was of a raccoon looking inquisitively from behind
a tree stump.

"How unusual!" She sat down and reached for the basket, running her fingers over the smooth, intricate carving.
"Such precise, delicate work! Who does this?"

Ellie looked up at her shyly. "It's old man Jenkins."
She looked at Bill. "You remember him maybe from
church? That's the only place he ever goes. He always
keeps his hat on, even when he's home. There's somethin'
kinda wrong with his hair—it sorta grows in spots. Folks
laugh at it sometimes, so he keeps it covered all the time.
It's made him feel bad, so he don't like to meet folks. Guess
he's always been that way."

She looked down at the objects in Bill's hands and added,

"Because he don't talk much with words, I guess he talks with these."

Mrs. Andrews looked up, startled by Ellie's perceptiveness. How could she know that, as young and simple as she was? She frowned uncertainly at the thoughts that were pushing at her, making her wonder about herself and the rightness of her ideas.

"Would he sell me some of these?" she asked finally, out of the confusion of her thoughts.

Ellie shook her head doubtfully. "I don't rightly know. He ain't never has. He just makes 'em for something to do 'cause he don't do much else. It sort of fills in time for him."

"Would you ask him?" Bill urged.

"I guess I could," Ellie answered, still hesitating.

"Does he have a lot of these already made?" Mrs. Andrews turned the salad bowl around in her hands as she asked. "I'd like to send a half dozen to Emily," she explained to Bill. "I had given up the idea of Christmas gifts for them because there was no opportunity to buy anything. But these would be just right."

Ellie nodded her head vigorously. "Oh, he works fast. It wouldn't take him no time at all to make 'em." She hesitated a moment and then added, "But he might think you was just foolin,' though, askin' to buy some. He just gives 'em away mostly, if folks want 'em."

"Does he make other kinds of things?"

Ellie nodded again. "He's got things all over. He has to shove 'em over so there's room on the table to eat."

"Would he let me come in and see them?"

Ellie shook her head slowly. "He's scared of folks he don't know. Thinks they'll laugh at him."

"You know we wouldn't make fun of him," Bill said seriously. "Would you go to his house with my mother? Then he'll know she's a person to be trusted. If he knows she's your friend, he won't be afraid of her."

Ellie gave a swift, scared glance up at Mrs. Andrews' face and then ducked her head. "If it wasn't that he lived up the ridge so far, we could maybe push you in your chair," she said in a small voice.

The reason for her reluctance was so obvious that Mrs. Andrews shifted uncomfortably but with some irritation. She had not been that unkind to the girl, surely, to make her actually afraid!

She forced herself to say gently, "Ellie, this is such beautiful work, I would be very happy to buy some pieces to send as gifts. You would be doing your friend a kindness by helping him sell them. Perhaps you could help me pick out something Peggy might like."

After a moment Ellie nodded and stood up. "We can go right now if you want," she offered. "I come real early to work this morning so I can get off now. He'll likely be there, 'cause he never goes no place."

They walked together up the hill, following a path that branched off to circle the ridge behind the town. Ellie stopped at the little house standing by itself at the end of the path and knocked. Then she opened the door calling, "Mr. Jenkins? It's me. Ellie. Me and—" She stopped and glanced at Mrs. Andrews. "Me and a friend. Can we see your pretties?"

"Walk in."

The man sitting at the table with his back to them did not look around as they entered, and Mrs. Andrews stared around in amazement. What Ellie had said about carvings being all over was true. There was not a level surface that was not filled with pieces of wood either already carved, or partly finished, or ready to be started. The wood gave a pungent smell to the room, not exactly unpleasant, but certainly very noticeable.

"This here's a lady who wants to get some of your things. Can she look around?"

"She's in, ain't she?" was the gruff reply.

Mrs. Andrews, examining the delicate carvings lying so carelessly around, was too absorbed to notice him. She found it hard to make a choice, for picking up one piece revealed another even more intriguing. When she had finally decided on a number of items, he refused to set a price but bent over his work, not even looking around at her. She finally laid on the table beside him some money, which he did not even look at.

She worried about it as she walked with Ellie back down the rough path to the road leading back to the hospital.

"Ellie, do you think I gave him a fair price?"

Ellie stopped in the path and looked at her, her eyes wide with surprise. "You are asking what *I* think?"

"Why yes. I haven't had any experience in knowing how valuable these might be. I certainly do not want to take advantage of him."

"He ain't never had no pay for those things, so it ain't likely he'll think you cheated him. But I'm proud you asked my view."

"I needed your advice, since you are at home here and know the customs." Mrs. Andrews hesitated, giving a quick, sidelong glance at Ellie. "We are the outsiders, you know, Ellie. Bill and I. It's not easy to become acquainted with people and their customs in a different part of the country. Every place has its own way of doing things. Since we are here for just a short time and will probably never come back, we might not understand your ways. And, of course, a person from here would find our ways strange and hard to adjust to."

There, she thought. *I've said what needed to be said out of kindness for the girl. She shouldn't go on setting her heart on something that's impossible for her to have. Better for her to be hurt now than later.*

Ellie walked along beside her without answering, her head bent and the ends of the long scarf around her throat blowing up to shield her face.

A guilty feeling nagged at Mrs. Andrews, and she reacted against it with impatience. There was no reason for the feeling. She was only doing her duty to the girl and trying to help her.

"I'll buy her a pretty blouse or sweater as a Christmas gift when I go to Louisville Saturday to meet Peggy," she decided.

On Saturday, the inexplicable feeling that she somehow had to atone to Ellie made her buy a long-sleeved, cuffed, print blouse; a coordinated sweater set to match; and a long, gold chain, spending more for her gifts than for those she bought Peggy.

After shopping she had lunch and then browsed through the stores until time to go to the bus station where Peggy had said her friends would drop her. She was early and sat watching the crowds milling back and forth through the waiting room, wondering about them and their family situations. All of them were different, no doubt—some happy, some not. *Like our family.*

Memories were painful, and she pushed them away, straightening her shoulders against the back of the hard wooden bench. She glanced at her watch and then looked up as Peggy dropped her suitcases on the floor and bent to hug her.

"Mother! It's great to see you! I'd like you to meet my friends. They insisted on parking and coming in to be sure I wasn't being left here alone. I told them I could count on you being here in plenty of time."

When they were finally on the bus and out on the road toward town, Peggy asked, "How is Bill really, Mother? Is he thinner? Or maybe fatter from doing nothing all these weeks?"

"Doing nothing, indeed! It's hard work to learn to walk again—and talk. The speech has come back fully, long ago. You won't be able to appreciate the hard work that took, since you did not hear how slow and slurred his words were at first. He is almost recovered in every way and will be walking normally soon."

"That *is* hard for me to believe," Peggy admitted. "When I remember what he looked like before I left—I was really afraid he would never come out of it!"

"I never doubted it. Not for an instant." Mrs. Andrews' voice was crisp. "I was determined that by both of us working together he would recover."

Peggy didn't answer. As she stared out the bus window, the worry that had been part of her thoughts all fall crystallized. She had been afraid her mother would see Bill's recovery as something she had accomplished in spite of God, not because of Him. The accident would be God's fault; Bill's recovery her doing. And instead of the whole experience drawing her to God, it would drive her farther away.

Her mind worried over the situation as she answered her mother's questions about school and people with only surface attention.

"I'd forgotten what it looked like here," she said as the bus wound along the road through the grayness of the late afternoon. "I remember the color and beauty of everything, since it was still summer when we were here. But now it looks different. It's kind of spooky the way the mist floats around like that. What is it? Fog?"

"I suppose so. It's like this from late afternoon until well after the sun rises in the morning. This time of the year is the worst, apparently. It was pretty when the leaves were turning." She leaned forward to peer out the window. "Well, here we are."

The bus pulled to a stop in front of the tiny cafe which was also the bus station, and Peggy rapped eagerly on the window as she saw Bill.

He waved in response, and she saw his lips move with words she could not hear.

Ellie stood behind him, her hands gripping the back of the chair and a shy smile touching her lips as she watched Peggy jump off the bus steps and lean to hug Bill.

"What a loafer you are! Not even gentleman enough to stand up to meet me!" Peggy scolded affectionately. Then she brushed at the tears in her eyes. "Sorry to be so emotional. But when I remember how you looked the last time I saw you—"

"Yeah. And I'm really disappointed to still be in this chair. I'm not in it much anymore. But Ellie and I decided to use it because some of the road is pretty rough to manage on crutches, and we didn't want to be late with our welcoming committee."

Peggy smiled at Ellie. "I feel as though I know you. Bill has written so much about you and says he owes a lot of his recovery to you."

Before Ellie could answer, Mrs. Andrews interrupted with a brisk, "We'd better go along while it's still light. We're all to have supper at your grandmother's, isn't that right, Ellie? Does she need you ahead of time to help?"

Ellie began to stammer a reply, but Bill interrupted smoothly. "No, we stopped on the way down to see if there was anything to be done. Here, Peg, put that suitcase by my feet and that big one on my lap. I guess you'll have to carry that one. How long are you staying, anyway, bringing so much stuff?"

"I could have left the one with the Christmas presents at school," she retorted.

"If that's this big one, I'll hang on to it. Peggy, you can push if you're strong enough. If not, Ellie will, because she's had practice."

He stopped talking and grinned up at them. "Boy, this is great! Me ordering three women around."

"Just wait till you get back on your feet, and see how long we jump to obey," Peggy answered. "Ellie, show me how to keep this thing straight with such a heavy load."

They moved along the road, Ellie and Peggy both pushing the chair and laughing at Bill's directions. Mrs. Andrews followed as they walked in the mist of the early evening which surrounded them and muted the sound of their voices.

8

A Painful Conversation

THEY WALKED QUICKLY in the gray chill of the late afternoon dusk. When they reached the porch, with its one low step, Mrs. Andrews gave directions about turning the chair and backing it up onto the porch. In the open doorway Mrs. Withrow stood framed by the light from the kitchen, the cooking smells floating out invitingly.

Bill put his head back and took a deep breath. "Umm. Why doesn't dinner at the hospital smell this good?"

"Because that cook's got outlandish ideas about what she calls nutrition. Instead of just cookin' up things that taste good so they're bound to *be* good for a person, she balances one thing 'gainst another. And usually all it ends up as is a mess."

Her sharp voice stopped, and she looked at them grouped on the porch. "Well, come in." Her glance swept Peggy. "I'd a known you for Bill's sister anywhere. You look just alike."

"I'm prettier than he is, I hope," Peggy answered with a smile turning up the corners of her mouth.

"Pretty is as pretty does," Mrs. Withrow retorted. She looked across the room at Ellie. "Show her where she's to sleep. And hurry down. The biscuits is 'bout ready."

Later, as they sat at the supper table, the uneasiness and anxiety Peggy had felt over this Christmas visit began to fade. Bill looked good and sounded as eager and enthusiastic and fun as he always had. Her mother—

Peggy looked across the table at her. She seemed relaxed—at home, even, though she sat somewhat on the fringe of the conversation. But she had been that way at Aunt Emily's, Peggy remembered. At least here she did not appear to be fighting against anything. Maybe, just maybe during the next two weeks there would be time for them to talk.

"What are we doing about a Christmas tree?" she asked as she and her mother walked to the hospital early the next morning. "Can we get a small one and put it up in Bill's room? Or are we joining Mrs. Withrow and Ellie?"

"We certainly are not going to impose on her," Mrs. Andrews answered emphatically. "I am too much in debt to her as it is."

"I don't suppose she thinks of it that way," Peggy protested. "She's just helping."

"That may well be, but I think we've been imposing. I don't intend to do it for a moment longer than necessary."

Her voice left no room for argument, and they finished the walk to the hospital in silence. As she watched her mother, Peggy could see there had been no softening in her independent attitude and idea of self-sufficiency. Again the hopelessness of her ever admitting her need of God swept over Peggy. If all these experiences did not drive her mother to God, what would?

She would not go to church with them that week; and Peggy, sitting through the informal service, could see how it would offend her mother's strong, inborn reserve. Peggy enjoyed the friendliness of the people, though she could sympathize with her mother, for some of the informality

was embarrassing to her. She admired the ease with which
Bill fit into the situation.

Ellie quickly lost her shyness with Peggy. She sat up in
bed that Sunday night, the blanket wrapped around her
slender shoulders, and watched Peggy do her nightly exercises.

"I was really feared of you coming."

"You shouldn't have been. You're not afraid of Bill,
and I'm just his sister."

"But he showed me your picture and told me about you.
How smart you are an' all. And I'd already seen you and
knew you was pretty."

Peggy dropped her arms to her sides as she straightened
up and looked across the room at Ellie's wide blue eyes
framed by the mass of hair growing back in a wave from
her forehead.

"Thank you, Ellie! Nobody ever said that to me before
and meant it so much. And there've been lots of times I
wished someone would! I really am very ordinary looking.
You should see the girl who lives across the hall from me."

"But it's—it's everything about you," Ellie went on, her
slim fingers pulling at a thread at the edge of the blanket.
"You're from the outside. I've never been out of this one
place in all my life. Oh, once my paw took me to Louisville. But I was real little, an' all I remember is the noise
an' the loud sounds and all the rushin' around folks did.
It was scary. I was real glad to get back home."

Peggy wrapped a blanket around her shoulders and sat
down, bracing her back comfortably against the foot of the
bed, her arms clasped around her bent knees. "It's not
where you live that matters, Ellie. It's who you are—what
you are like—"

Ellie interrupted, struggling for the words to express herself. "That's just why I was scared of you. I ain't even been much to school, and you go to college. I can't go on and be a nurse, a real one, I mean. I can only mop the floors and put on clean sheets."

"But those things are important to a patient, too. And it's the way they are done, cheerfully and with your pretty smile, that makes the difference."

The words sounded preachy in her ears, and she was sure they must to Ellie, too, as she shook her head and curled down in a small heap under the blankets. Watching her, Peggy remembered her mother's urging last evening that she find time to point out to Ellie how hopeless it was for her to think about Bill. *She knows that already. That's one reason she's so sad.*

There was really nothing anyone could do to help. This was something Ellie would have to fight through alone and accept. Remembering her own feelings about Larry in the long ago past, she knew what Ellie was suffering. The difference was that life really did not hold much promise for Ellie, while hers was so rich and full.

Long after Ellie fell asleep, Peggy lay awake thinking about the inequalities of life. *There must be something we can do to help her. God must have some purpose in letting us meet this way.*

At the breakfast table the next morning, Mrs. Withrow insisted that they have Christmas together, and Mrs. Andrews argued that they did not want to impose.

"The way I see it, you've only got two choices, here and the hospital. If you was to choose Christmas dinner at that place, I'd say you deserve what you get." Mrs. Withrow snapped her lips shut in an expression of contempt.

Mrs. Andrews finally agreed but insisted that they divide

the responsibility. If Mrs. Withrow would cook, she would pay the expenses.

They bought a Christmas tree and set it up in the tiny front room, improvising a holder for the tree trunk. Mrs. Withrow brought out a box of tree decorations from years past. Most of them were pine cones decorated with bits of ribbon. There were also delicate scraps of material, each piece shaped and tied in the center.

"Like butterflies," Ellie explained, buttoning herself into her coat to go to work.

"How clever," Peggy exclaimed, holding several up to the light from where she knelt on the floor. She jumped up and tied a half dozen on the tree branches and stood back to see the effect. "They *do* look like butterflies!"

"A little," Mrs. Andrews gave grudging agreement from the doorway.

The years fell away as Peggy looked at the scrawny little tree with its improvised ornaments. Other Christmases flashed through her memory. There were those of her child-hood years, when there had not been much money to spend. Most of the tree decorations then had been those she and Bill had made with their father's help while her mother regretted that there was not money for the glittering orna-ments displayed in the stores. Then came the miserable Christmas she had spent at Aunt Emily's. There the tree had sparkled with ornaments lined in precise rows among the shimmering tinsel so carefully layered by the dec-orator Aunt Emily had hired. There was the unhappy year when Jane had come to visit them, and all the dis-agreements between her parents had surfaced so plainly.

There had been happy times, of course, but these others were the ones that stood out so vividly. And this one with

Dad gone was the saddest of all. Blinking back the tears that threatened to come at the reminder of her father and the fun he had always put into the holiday, she went out to the kitchen.

Ellie had gone to work, and Mrs. Withrow had thrown her usual shawl around her thin, bent shoulders and had gone to help the neighbor who was so sick. The kitchen was warm, with the oven going and a stew bubbling gently on the stove. Mrs. Andrews had made gingerbread, and its spicy fragrance added to the coziness of the atmosphere.

"It's too bad Bill decided not to come down for supper since gingerbread is one of his favorites. How come he isn't?"

"I think he's finishing a Christmas gift he's making. We'd better not walk in on him without knocking when we go this evening."

"Things are more fun when he's around, aren't they?" Peggy exclaimed.

Her mother nodded. "That is why those first days of uncertainty were so difficult to endure. Especially when I knew even then—was sure when the news first came—" She stopped and turned her head away. "I was sure right from the first that—that your father—" She stopped again, and Peggy could see her lips trembling.

"Have you *really* missed him, Mother?" The question came impulsively, and all the doubt and fear and anxiety of her childhood was in her voice.

"Of course I miss him!" Mrs. Andrews turned to face Peggy, her hand clenched into a fist on the table between them. "What makes you ask a question like that?"

Peggy looked away from the hurt and anger in her mother's eyes. She could not tell her the many times she had wondered if her mother really loved her father. But Mrs. Andrews had not waited for an answer, and Peggy listened as her words poured out.

"One should never judge other people's marriage just by looking at it from the outside. No two people ever think exactly alike or react the same way to situations. Your father and I were from such different backgrounds. And perhaps I was less prepared for marriage than he, less ready to adapt to someone else, to yield my own wishes and plans when they were not important. I had been raised with so much comfort and ease. When I met your father and we were married, I—I thought love would be enough to live on if there was not enough money to buy the things I wanted—and thought I needed. And then I found love wasn't enough."

She looked across at Peggy. "It was not that I didn't love your father. We were very much in love. But people show love differently. And experience love in different depths. Some find it easy to say 'I'm sorry' or 'I love you.' Or even sometimes 'I need you.' Sometimes one doesn't realize the importance of saying those words—not just feeling them but *saying* them out loud—until it is too late." After a moment, in a low voice she added, "And then one lives with regret, and there is no way to make restitution. It's too late."

Peggy heard the ache in her mother's voice and struggled for the words that would comfort without excusing her for the words and actions that had been a hindrance to her through her growing years.

Finally, groping for the words, she said, "It doesn't matter to Dad now—where he is. He understands everything, and any hurts from this life are all gone." She hesitated, wondering how much to say in this moment when her mother's guard was down and she seemed more open.

"The Bible says, 'God shall wipe away all tears from their eyes; and there shall be no more death, neither sorrow, nor crying,' for those who belong to God. Dad belonged to God while he was living, and he does even more so now."

She wanted to add, "Won't you accept Christ and belong to God, too?" But the fear of antagonizing her mother stopped the words.

In the silence between them, they could hear the wind sifting through the trees and blowing up against the house as though trying to find a way in. A song rang in Peggy's ears, one that had been sung in church that last Sunday she was home alone before going to college. It had stayed with her through the months at school, and the words came back now in snatches.

> Some day you'll hear God's final call . . .
> His offer of salvation . . .
> This could be it . . .
> God's final call . . .
>
> If you reject God's final call . . .
> You'll have no chance . . .
> All hope will then be gone . . .
> Oh, hear His call. *

The words, carrying their haunting finality of invitation, were so vivid in her mind that she said them aloud without realizing it until she heard the echo of her voice. She looked across the table at her mother who sat motionless, her hands gripped tightly together.

She watched her mother stand up suddenly without a

*GOD'S FINAL CALL, © 1961 by Singspiration, Inc. All rights reserved. Used by permission.

word and go upstairs. Peggy listened to the sound of the bedroom door shutting, closing out any more contact. How often through the years her mother had done this, simply refusing to discuss what she did not want to acknowledge.

The late afternoon quietly ticked away with the clock. Mrs. Withrow came in briefly to say she would not be home to eat until late because her neighbor still needed her. When Ellie came home for supper, Peggy went up to knock at her mother's door, and listened to the answer she called through the closed door.

"Peggy, I'm very tired. If you don't mind going to the hospital alone, I'm simply going to bed to get rested."

"Can't I bring you some dinner on a tray? The stew smells delicious."

"No, I'm quite all right. I won't want anything until morning. Don't alarm Bill about my not coming. There is nothing wrong. I'm just unusually tired."

Peggy set the table for herself and Ellie and tried to carry on a conversation, though she could talk with only surface attention. Her mind kept traveling back over her mother's words and her own ineptness. She had really spoiled things, and her mother's mind was as closed as ever.

Ellie offered to walk back with her to visit Bill, and Peggy looked at her gratefully. "Oh, Ellie, would you? You don't mind after working all day?"

Ellie shook her head. "I've not had so much fun in my whole life as havin' you an' Bill here. I'm sure goin' to miss you all when you go. Seems like you and him are easier to talk to than anyone else I ever knew. It's goin' to be mighty lonesome around here when you go."

Peggy reached to squeeze her hand at the sadness in her voice. "You'll have to come visit me at school," she said impulsively. "The girls on my floor are always doubling up so someone can have a friend sleep in. You could come for a weekend sometime. It would be fun having you."

Ellie shook her head. "I couldn't. I'd be too scared. Everyone would be so smart and—"

"But, Ellie, you'd be my friend."

She shook her head again. "Not everyone would be like you. And anyway, even if they was, I'd—I'd feel funny. I couldn't talk to anybody. Maybe I couldn't even talk right to you there. Here—well, here it's different. Here is home. I belong."

They had reached the hospital, and Peggy didn't argue. Ellie was right. She would feel out of place. Maybe in time she would adjust to the differences, but a weekend visit would only make her more conscious of what she did not have.

Bill was waiting for them just inside the front door in the lobby and turned to push himself on his crutches along the hall with them, talking excitedly.

"A big package—box, really—came from California this afternoon. They delivered it here. And there's a letter from Jane. She said to open it right away and take out the things that weren't wrapped because they're not Christmas presents. I guess they thought the box would get here sooner than it did. Just look at the size of it!"

Bill pushed open the door of his room and let them enter, as he asked, "Didn't Mother come?"

Peggy shook her head. "She was awfully tired and decided to go to bed early."

She did not want to say anything more in Ellie's hearing. The box had come at just the right time to lift her spirits from the despair she felt over her mother and the sadness at Ellie's narrow life.

Could this be just a coincidence or God's timing? And

if it was His timing in such a trivial matter, couldn't she trust His timing in such an important matter as her mother's salvation? She could, of course. But the awful thought persisted that her mother could refuse until the final call stopped.

Bill's eager voice broke through her sad thoughts. "Let's go ahead and open it," he urged, and pulled a chair over by the box and lowered himself onto it. "Come on, Ellie, you and Peggy work at that rope on that side, and I'll get this knot untied."

When the wrappings were finally torn away, they lifted out package after package. Some were addressed to Ellie and her grandmother also. There were several games, "to be used now," Jane had written across the tops of the boxes, and a set of weights for Bill. Candy and nuts and fruitcake were also included.

"They sure must be rich!" Ellie said, as she looked around at the pile of packages. "And look at them fancy wrappings and beautiful ribbons. I never thought anybody could spend so much just on givin' presents."

"Lots of people do, Ellie."

"Not here. No one here could. Folks here need their money just for livin'. It's—it's scary to know folks can spend so much just on presents."

Ellie seemed to retreat from them in her words, and Peggy reached toward her.

"Ellie, we could never spend money like this. Please don't let this bother you. Yes, our relatives are rich. Maybe they shouldn't spend so much money just on gifts, but they can afford it. Just accept whatever they've sent you and your grandmother because it comes with love."

"But they don't know us."

"That doesn't matter. They know how kind you've been

to us. We couldn't have gotten along without you these months. This is their way of helping us say thanks."

"Grandma—she don't take kindly to accepting things. Specially from folks she don't know."

"Yes, she is like that. Some people know how to give but not to take. Your grandmother is one of them."

"We've got another problem to think of first," Bill broke in. "That's how to get all this stuff down to your grandmother's. Then we'll worry about whether she'll accept them."

"That's no problem," Peggy retorted. "Tomorrow we'll just pile them all in your wheelchair, and let you hop along on your crutches."

"Good idea! After all, if I'm expecting to leave here in three weeks and get back in school, I've got to get rid of this chair for good."

"Three weeks! Bill, don't—don't count on that!"

He looked down at her as she sat on the floor surrounded by packages, staring up at him in alarm. "Of course I can, Peg. That's the prayer I wake up with in the morning and go to sleep with at night."

"Bill—God may have other plans." She hated to dampen his enthusiasm, but she was older. She had an obligation to help him face his situation realistically. Three weeks was too soon.

He interrupted her, leaning forward in his intensity. "Peggy, I've thought about all that. I've already faced wondering what God's will was when I came to and realized what bad shape I was in. I couldn't figure it all out. I'd known for a long time that God wanted me to preach. And by the end of the summer I was pretty sure it might be here in the hills. I tried to figure out how I could do it if I were crippled. It would be hard to go to school and then get a church and visit people. So after a while I was sure I was going to get over this. That it would just be a question of how soon."

He stopped, looking at them in the quiet of the dimly lit room. "I knew God could do a miracle and heal me in a minute. But I figured there wasn't any need for Him to do it that way as long as I could help myself some. So I prayed mornings that I would be able to stretch a little farther on the exercise bars that day and walk a little longer with my crutches. Every night I thanked God that He'd helped me. It's just plain common sense to do what you can and then ask God to do what you can't."

"Bill—will that work for Mother, too?" Peggy's voice was urgent in its question.

"I don't see why not. Look how we've prayed for her. That's our part. Someday God will do His part and answer our prayer. It's just a question of how soon."

The memory of her mother's bedroom door closing her off faded as Peggy looked back at Bill's confident face.

9

Christmas Eve

BILL DID WALK down the rough, gravelled, winding hospital drive the next day, swinging himself along on his crutches slowly at first and then faster as he gained confidence. The girls pushed the chair ahead of him along the narrow street through town, sitting down once on a bench in front of one of the stores to give not only Bill a chance to rest but themselves also. They had laughed so much trying to ignore the stares of people they passed as they manipulated the wheelchair full of packages that they both felt weak.

"You're taking your whole lunch hour to do this, though, Ellie," Peggy protested as they started on again. "I hate to take all your time. I can manage it the rest of the way."

Ellie shook her head. "This is lots more fun than eating all alone at the hospital. I'll get me a biscuit at Granny's an' eat it on the way back. She'll likely not be there, or she'd think I ought to set down and eat proper."

When they had finally arrived at the house and had carried in all the packages, Peggy saw Ellie's wistful face as she turned reluctantly to leave, looking back over her shoulder at the two of them and Mrs. Andrews as they sat around the kitchen table talking.

"We'll wait with everything until you get back, Ellie. We won't do a thing to the tree until you get home."

When Ellie had gone, Bill swung himself across the

107

kitchen to the stack of packages just inside the small parlor
and came back with a box tucked under his arm as he held
onto the crutches.

"Peggy, wrap this for me while Ellie's gone, will you?
I didn't want to do it at the hospital in case she came in
unexpectedly and saw me. I could have pretended it was
for you, but I didn't want to lie. Anyway, she's already
wrapped yours from me."

He opened the box as he spoke and pulled out a matched
scarf and hat set as blue as the color of the fall sky.

"That's for Ellie?" Mrs. Andrews asked sharply. "I
thought you were making it for Peggy."

He shook his head. "I didn't think Peggy needed something that took so much work—"

"*You* made this?" Astonishment colored Peggy's voice.
"When—and where—did you learn? I didn't know you
could knit! Bill, this is *beautiful!*"

"Watching Mom gave me the idea. It took a long time.
But of course I had a lot of time, more of that than anything else. And it helped my fingers get their speed back
and be less clumsy in handling things. I knew I'd have to
type a lot of papers for school, and my fingers felt so stiff.
So I figured something like this would help. And at the
same time, it would give Ellie something pretty to wear.
The color matches her eyes, doesn't it? Mom picked the
color."

"Only when I thought you were making it for Peggy,"
his mother retorted. "What do you mean that Peggy doesn't
need something requiring so much work?"

"She doesn't, really. Not compared to Ellie." He looked
at Peggy, who nodded her understanding, and he went on.
"Ellie's not had much all her life. And she doesn't have
much to look forward to. I didn't want just to buy some-

thing, even if I'd known what to get. This way she'll know I really thought of her, and it will give her something to remember us by when we're gone."

"It's apt to give her a different idea altogether." Mrs. Andrew's voice was disapproving, and she looked across at Bill with a frown.

He looked back at his mother soberly. "Ellie knows more than you think, Mom." He frowned in thought. "Maybe a better word is *feels*. She knows lots of things by feeling."

Mrs. Andrews looked away without answering, oddly rebuked by the compassion and wisdom in Bill's young voice. Her lips firmed with determination. It was imperative that they get away from this atmosphere, back to the normalcy of their former lives. Yet she knew life would never be the same. Something vital had gone from it for her, something she had not known how much she treasured until now that it was gone forever. The sudden rush of grief so overwhelmed her that she hurried up to her bedroom with a muttered excuse of needing to wrap gifts. She felt herself shivering, partly from the chill in the room and partly from the turmoil of her emotions. As she walked back and forth across the room, hugging her arms against herself, her thoughts tumbled in confusion.

The disregard she had had toward God in her earlier life had gradually grown to impatience at those who found Him necessary in their lives, then to active dislike, and finally to anger at Him. But neither ignoring Him nor railing against Him had kept Him away. Instead, He had invaded her world everywhere she turned—through Peggy and Bill first, and then by entering her husband's life. Even Walter and finally Emily had found that all their money was not

enough, and they too talked about being saved. If all these
were right about God, it meant she was wrong.

She turned abruptly and dragged the rocking chair over
to the window and sat down, her hands gripping the worn
wooden arms as she rocked back and forth. Surely it was
just all the sentiment over Christmas that was upsetting her,
all the emotionalism of the past weeks and months. Once
she was back home, she would get a job to pay expenses
and would keep busy. She would have no time to think
morbid thoughts.

The afternoon passed as she sat by the window and
watched the sun slowly sink behind the hills. Ellie came
quickly along the narrow road and turned up the path to
the house, eagerness clear on her face. She heard the young
voices downstairs and smelled the fragrance of baking
bread.

Finally, reluctantly, driven only by the habit of years of
helping with the work, she stood up and crossed to the
dresser to comb her hair. The face that looked back
seemed old and— She leaned closer to the mirror in the
dim light. Severe! That was the word. Was she really?
Was this the way she looked to others?

Someone knocked on the door as she stared at herself
and Peggy called, "Mother? Did I leave my Bible in your
room?"

"Yes, just a minute." She turned back to the mirror and
reached to fluff her hair, pulling it more softly at the temples
and around her ears.

She picked up the Bible lying beside the small lamp on
the dresser and papers slipped out. As she shuffled them
together to slip them back in place, she saw the list of
names Peggy had written on the inside back page of her

Bible. Some she did not recognize, but others stood out—
Ellen, Dad, Mother, Uncle Walter, Aunt Emily, Jane,
Alice, Dan, Phyllis. Each name had a check beside it—all
but hers. She frowned as she stared down at the list. There
could be only one reason for the list, a reason she might not
have known if she had not just gone over some of the same
names herself. And her name was the only one without a
check mark beside it.

She closed the Bible, holding it tight in her two hands,
as she heard Peggy knock again; and she walked slowly to
the door and opened it.

Peggy looked at her, her eyes anxious, and beyond her
to the rocking chair by the window as she took the Bible.

"Ellie said her grandmother won't be home for supper
and that we should go ahead and eat. We're going to the
service at church tonight, you know. It's a special Christmas service."

Her voice ended on a questioning note as she followed
her mother down the narrow stairs to the kitchen. She
didn't ask, "Are you going?" but the question hung in the
air between them.

Mrs. Andrews merely said, "We'll see," and helped serve
the meal. The distaste she felt about the church and sitting
through another service grew as she listened to the conversation of the girls doing the dishes and Bill swinging himself back and forth on his crutches to put them away.

"I'll stay home and wait for your grandmother," she said
to Ellie with sudden decision, glad for the valid excuse that
Peggy could not argue against. "She will be hungry and
tired. She's kept a cup of tea ready for me a number of
times these past weeks when I've come in tired. This will
give me a chance to repay her kindness."

"Granny sure won't be expecting nothing like that," Ellie replied. "But it's right kind of you," she added with a shy smile.

When they had gone, with Bill insisting he would walk if they didn't go too fast, the house seemed empty. She went to the doorway of the parlor and looked at the tree decorated with the homemade ornaments and the strings of cranberries and popcorn that had been the reason for all the laughter in the kitchen. How silly to be sentimental over it. It was a very ordinary tree, without even any lights to sparkle it. She crossed to the one small lamp on the end table near the tree and tilted the shade so that the light reflected on the red berries and the few shiny ornaments spotted here and there. Then she went back to the kitchen and moved Mrs. Withrow's big rocking chair into a place where she could see the tree and sat down. The room was warm from the stove where a teakettle of water simmered slowly, a gentle mist of steam escaping from the spout.

Presently she heard footsteps on the porch. Mrs. Withrow pushed open the door, letting in a current of air that whisked through the room and curled around Mrs. Andrews' ankles.

"Saw the light and thought likely it would be you." Mrs. Withrow's comment was matter-of-fact as she hung her shawl on the hook by the door.

Mrs. Andrews stood up, shoving the rocking chair back in place. "You'll have some tea?" she asked and turned to the cupboard for two cups and saucers.

"I need something to take the chill out of my bones and my spirit," Mrs. Withrow replied. "This is a special time, being it's Christmas Eve. Calls for a bit of celebrating."

She went into the parlor and came back with two thin cups and saucers and two tiny, worn-thin silver spoons.

"They're all that's left from a set that come over on a ship with my ancestors years back. They was more, but what with packin' and unpackin', being put in and out of barrels, jolted across mountain passes in wagons, washed by careless hands now and then, this is all that's left."

"How beautiful!" Mrs. Andrews held up one of the cups so that light shone through the fragile china.

Mrs. Withrow cradled one of the thin cups in both work-rough hands. "I don't use 'em often; but when I do, I can't help thinkin' of the stories they could spin, the sights they've seen, the places my mind can't never imagine."

Her voice was thin and wispy, as though it came itself from the dim past of which it spoke. "They always talk to me of a different world—one I ain't never seen and never will. A world of beauty."

Slight impatience was clear in Mrs. Andrews' voice as she said briskly, "A cup is a cup, and what it's made of doesn't change the taste of what's put in it."

"Sometimes, if the tea's bitter, it goes down easier if it's surrounded by a bit of beauty," Mrs. Withrow answered in the same far-off voice, still holding the delicate cup tenderly.

"Is there something you would like with your tea? We saved you some supper." Mrs. Andrews deliberately made her voice clear and crisp to break the spell of the moment.

Mrs. Withrow shook her head. "Nothing but a bite of that bread and some honey and cheese to go with it."

Mrs. Andrews heard the weariness dragging her voice and looked across at her sympathetically. "You're tired."

She nodded. "My neighbor. She's goin' to leave seven younguns to be farmed out to relatives. Too bad to split a family like that. Things won't never be the same again for 'em."

"What about her husband?"

Mrs. Withrow shrugged. "He'll likely remarry. A man can't get along by himself the way a woman can. He needs someone to cook his meals, manage the house. When a woman's left alone, if her kids is old enough, she can make herself a new life. 'Course somethin's gone, especially if there's been love. That can't never be replaced the same as before."

She sipped her tea and then shook her head sorrowfully as she added, "All I could think to say to my neighbor was, God knows. Not one sparrow falls to the ground—"

"But they do all the time!" Mrs. Andrews could not check her scornful interruption.

"It don't say they won't fall. But it says when they do, God sees it. He knows about it. And He's there to help. It don't make no difference what happens to folks as long as they've got God."

She looked across at Mrs. Andrews then and spoke directly. "We was talkin' about bitter tea a while back. Find yourself some beautiful cup for the rest of your life, and it won't seem so hard and bitter."

"It's always been bitter, regardless of the cup."

"Has it, now?" The surprise was so strong in Mrs. Withrow's voice and eyes that Mrs. Andrews looked away from her. "I wouldn't of thought that. Why, you've had the love of a fine husband from the talk I hear of him from Bill. Your daughter is sweet; your son, gentle and kind. What is it you need to sweeten your life?"

"You have no right to sit in judgment when you don't know the whole story," she flashed back.

"I ain't judging. Maybe you've had it harder than it looks. I don't know. But from what I've seen, if a woman's got the love of a good man and the love of obedient younguns, whatever else she don't have don't much matter. You can stand not havin' money or a fancy house—even poor health ain't so bad if you know you're loved by the folks dearest to you."

She rocked a moment and then added, " 'Course, you need God's love, too. But any woman can have that, even the poor souls that don't have any other kind of love. But you—my stars, you can have all three kinds. Must be the only reason you got bitterness is because you let yourself have it. If that's so, you only got yourself to blame."

As she sat across the table from the level gaze and heard the quiet, accusing words that summed up all her discontent and grievances and dismissed them as trivial, it was only the habit of years of politeness that kept Mrs. Andrews from lashing out in reply. Mrs. Withrow was an interfering old busybody, preaching at her this way.

She doesn't know anything about the heartbreak of my life with Emily, the disappointment of being poor, John's faults. It was easy to talk about love glibly, but Mrs. Andrews had never found it sufficient to cover inadequacies. *It would have been enough if you had let it.* The thought was a faint whisper that only added to her anger and her need to justify herself.

She looked across at Mrs. Withrow with cold disdain, seeing her bent figure, her worn clothes, her rough, chapped hands and broken nails. She was nothing but an interfering busybody who preached at other people when she had not done a very good job with her own family. How could she talk this way with her husband dead years ago; her son killed in a drunken brawl; her granddaughter a delicate, needing-protection child whose future was so uncertain? What would become of Ellie when she died?

Suddenly, looking at the worn, lined face opposite her,

Mrs. Andrews felt the bitterness drain from her. This must be the fear at which Mrs. Withrow stared as she thought of her neighbor leaving young children to the mercy of other people. *What will become of Ellie* must be the thought that burdened each of her days.

"She could live with us."

She looked across at Mrs. Withrow, the words standing in the air between them. Her voice still echoed in her ears. She had said those words—and knew she had meant them.

"You can count on Ellie having a home with us if she needs it," she repeated and watched Mrs. Withrow's mouth begin to tremble. Her hands shook slightly as she put the cup and saucer she was holding carefully on the table.

Then she folded her hands in her lap and took a deep breath before she answered, her words coming slowly as though she felt her way along.

"You are a good woman, and I thank you kindly for thinkin' of Ellie—and me. You've been a good mother. I see that in your younguns. They wouldn't of turned out like they have if you hadn't of raised 'em right. I know you would do right by my Ellie in feedin' and clothin' her. I don't aim to seem ungrateful."

She hesitated, groping still for words. "But Ellie's special. She needs more than food and somethin' fittin' to wear. She needs special loving. Heart loving."

She stopped and said no more. But Mrs. Andrews knew the thought she had not spoken: *And I ain't sure you can give her that kind of love.*

The sound of voices outside the door ended the conversation. The commotion of getting Bill back to the hospital pushed it to the back of her mind, but Mrs. Withrow's unspoken thought nagged at her accusingly—and angered her.

Her love was not the mushy, sentimental kind. It was

sensible, seeing faults and pointing them out when necessary. Perhaps she was even critical at times—yes, she would admit that. But her criticism, though honest and frank, was never malicious.

Some people might get emotional over Ellie and *talk* about loving her. And even talk about praying for her, her mind argued defiantly. But that did not mean they would take her into their home and really take the responsibility for her.

Her offer had been impulsive; but, for some obscure reason she could not put into words even to herself now, she knew she had meant it. She wanted to look after Ellie. There was an urgent need in her to do something to help erase the anxiety from the face and heart of Mrs. Withrow.

Next year she would have to make a new life for herself. Bill would be in college, and life would be lonely. She had no really close friends who could fill the loss she would feel back in her familiar surroundings. She would have no one. *Except God, if I want Him,* came the whispered thought.

The thought kept her awake until far into the night, as she turned over and over in her mind the fact that all her life she had carried on a quarrel with God. Inescapable logic told her that she was the loser.

It was light when she finally wakened, not feeling rested or ready for this Christmas day. She heard Peggy and Ellie in the next room, their voices soft in conversation but with occasional giggles breaking through. Mrs. Withrow was obviously up, for the fragrance of coffee floated up the stairs invitingly. She felt guilty to be lying still in bed, when other Christmases she had had the responsibility of running the day smoothly.

"Other Christmases" seemed to be the theme running through most of the day, as first Peggy and then Bill would speak of something from the past with a laughing, "Do you remember the time we—?"

"Didn't you never have any unhappy times?" Ellie asked once, and Bill answered promptly, "If we did, I can't remember them. Not *really* unhappy ones."

Peggy did not answer. She looked across the room at her mother, sitting aloof, and worried about her, sure that there was no possibility of breaking through her reserve. This was the wrong atmosphere for her. There was not enough to stimulate her in this shut-off-from-the-world area. She needed to be with people she would consider her equals, women who were educated and cultured, women she could respect. There was no chance that she would ever listen to Mrs. Withrow who was so different.

I'll write Mrs. Parker and get her to introduce Mother to someone when she goes home. Maybe she knows women who are really sharp Christians who can be friends to Mother and reach her. It just won't work here!

Peggy's thoughts were somber as she sat with the rest of the family in the early dusk of evening, a cup of hot chocolate warming her hands but nothing, even on this wonderful Christmas day, to warm her heart. The hope of her mother's salvation had never beat so dimly as it did here in this small house with wind sighing through the trees outside and a scattering of snow whitening the hills. The cold and gloom of the outside pressed in to threaten the warmth of Bill's and Ellie's laughter, the tray of hot chocolate and cookies Mrs. Withrow brought in, her eager anticipation of Dan's coming.

The fullness of her own life contrasted so sharply with her mother's narrowed existence, made narrower now with Dad gone. The years of praying for her mother focused into this point in time and seemed utterly hopeless. Other answers to prayer marched before her: Dad, Alice, Ellen, Uncle Walter and Aunt Emily, Jane, Phyllis, Dan, Sally. But for none of them had the burden been so heavy or seemed so hopeless as this one she had carried for her mother through the years.

The words of the song came again in warning—"If you reject God's final call . . . you'll have no chance—"

No! She would not give up. God's final call to her mother would not come as long as she held onto Him in prayer.

10

Two Miracles

"NOW THAT CHRISTMAS is out of the way, Peggy can get down to the really important business of this vacation—waiting for Dan to come."

Bill grinned up at Peggy as he spoke, and she wrinkled her nose back at him.

"Wait'll he comes," she retorted. "I'll get him to really beat you at chess. He can do it, too."

"Maybe. But don't forget, I've gotten better at it. I'll bet I've played more this year than he has."

"He comes when? Monday?" Mrs. Andrews asked. "You will need to reserve a place for him to stay. Make a reservation at the motel and pay for it in advance. I'll give you the money."

"He won't want us to pay for it," Peggy protested. "He'll want to do it himself."

"Nevertheless, he is visiting us," her mother answered tartly. "Therefore he is our responsibility to care for."

"You make him sound like such a burden," Peggy protested.

The anxieties she had been feeling about Dan's coming surfaced again. Their own relationship at this point was thin from being nourished over the months only by letters. She knew her mother had never liked him, a feeling that went back through the years to the time they had first met and Dan's parents had fallen so far short of Mrs. Andrews' standards of friendship because of their poor clothes and broken English.

Peggy knew her mother would be very correct to Dan, but it would be a cold politeness that he would feel. She was not sure that he had enough strength to take that in stride without taking offense. She knew from his letters that God had warmed his nature a lot in the last months, but there was too much of the insecurity of his childhood still in him. She did not want him hurt needlessly. He was too important to her.

Her thoughts were interrupted by her mother's stern impatience. "Peggy, please don't misinterpret everything I say about this young man. If we were home and a guest came to visit, he would stay with us. Since we are not in our own home, we have to make the best arrangements we can. Dan obviously cannot stay either at the hospital or at Mrs. Withrow's. Therefore the motel is the only place left. Since he is our guest, we will pay his expenses. It is as simple as that, so please do not read into it any neglect or dislike of him on my part."

"But he can be with us all the rest of the time, can't he? For meals and other times, I mean?"

"Certainly."

"When do you go back?" Bill broke in.

"Probably really early in the morning the day after New Year's. I've got an eight o'clock class on the third that I can't miss."

"How long a drive is it?"

"About eight hours. But then Dan's got about four or five more to go. I hate for him to do it, but he wants to."

Mrs. Andrews looked across at Peggy, hearing the lilt

of her voice and seeing the happiness on her face. Her lips tightened in disapproval. It was because of Dan, of course.

But as she looked at Peggy and Bill laughing at one another across the checker board, she knew it was more than that. Peggy did not really seem to need either people or things to be happy. And Bill's eagerness and anticipation of life had not dimmed during the long months of recovery. Even initially facing the prospect of not ever walking again, he had kept an inner happiness that had buoyed him.

She was swept with a sudden urgent longing to have their joy for herself. Oh, she had known happiness, of course. Life had not been all bitterness and regret for the things she did not have. But the happiness had depended on so many other factors that it had never remained with her. What her children had, what John had had, seemed constant. Though she pushed the thought away, it came back to face her squarely. The source of happiness for Peggy and Bill was God.

The realization stayed with her the rest of the day and as she got ready for bed. The problem was that having ignored God all her life, it would be difficult now to admit her need. It was not easy to believe in God when she had fought against Him all her life. But her defences were rapidly crumbling. Something was pushing hard against all the closed doors inside her.

She walked restlessly around the room, feeling hemmed in by its narrowness and chilled by the night air that sifted in around the ill-fitting window frame. She tried rocking, remembering Mrs. Withrow's repeated, "Times a body needs to get rid of problems, rockin' helps."

But she found herself moving the chair faster and faster in time with the churning of her thoughts. As her own barriers crumbled, she was haunted by another thought. How could she have any assurance that God would be interested in her now, after all these years of her refusal of Him?

There was no one she could ask for help. She could not talk to either Peggy or Bill—not yet anyway, when she was not sure what she wanted to know. Emily and Walter were too far away, even if she were willing to humble herself sufficiently to ask their help. She was not ready for that yet, not desperate enough—probably would never be.

That left only Mrs. Withrow. She thought of the old woman, her abrupt, uncompromising, unsentimental way of speaking. She would give an honest answer. There was that unexpected bond between them in spite of differences in background and culture and education and opinions. If there were an opportunity before she and Bill left—she would not actively seek one out—but, if an opening came naturally, she would ask Mrs. Withrow her question.

With that settled, she went to bed and pulled the covers up securely around her, shutting out both the past and present.

She shook her head in a determined *no* Sunday morning when Peggy urged her to go to church with them, turning her head from the hopeful plea in Peggy's eyes. There was no answer to her question in the church service, she was sure.

She looked across the breakfast table at the girls. "Are you walking up to get Bill?"

Peggy shook her head. "No. He wants to come by himself, so we're meeting him at church."

"Is that wise?" Mrs. Andrews asked, her voice sharp with concern. "If the streets are slick— Is he coming in his chair?"

"No, on his crutches. And he says he can do it."

"I've been out. Things is dry," Mrs. Withrow spoke over her shoulder from the stove. "Turn him loose," she advised.

Mrs. Andrews thinned her lips in exasperation and ignored Mrs. Withrow's comment as she said to Peggy, "While you're gone, I'm going to the hospital to begin to gather up some of the things Bill has accumulated. We may have to mail some of them home when we are ready to leave. I want the packing properly cared for and not rushed at the last minute."

"I'll help you this afternoon," Peggy began, but Mrs. Andrews shook her head.

"I know just how I want it done and would rather do it alone."

She waited until she was sure they would be in the church building, and then walked rapidly along the streets and up the drive to the hospital. The very briskness of her walk and the anticipation of something definite to do gave purpose to the day. Thankfully, Ellie had the day off and was at church, so she would not be there to offer timid suggestions.

She walked confidently up the stairs and pushed open the door to Bill's room, wondering how many more times she would have to enter the room. Then thankfulness swept her as she thought of how far they had come since the first time she had entered to see Bill lying motionless and unaware.

Working quickly, she consolidated and packed and sorted, taking gifts out of boxes to conserve space. When the wastebasket was full, she picked it up and went along the hall to the bin at the far end, where she had seen Ellie empty the room baskets. Turning to come back, she almost collided with the doctor coming out of one of the rooms.

"Mrs. Andrews! I left word at the front desk that I wanted to see you. They must have missed you when you came in."

"Yes, I came about forty-five minutes ago and didn't speak to anyone."

"Have you time to stop in my office a few minutes?"

"Of course." She followed him, feeling her pulse quicken in anticipation of what he might say.

He motioned her to a chair and sat down facing her, his hands loosely folded in front of him on top of the desk. He smiled at her.

"I have good news for you. Much better news than I hoped for when I first saw your young man when he was brought in. I must say, I thought his chances of even living were very dim. And to think he might recover completely—well, that seemed remote at the time. But he has made such rapid strides, particularly in the last month, that I am really amazed. After studying his X-rays and the results of a battery of tests we've run on him, I see no reason why he cannot be released very soon, perhaps even in a week."

Mrs. Andrews caught her breath. "You're sure?"

The doctor nodded. "I've been in consultation with several doctors from the hospital in Louisville, and they agree. Give him a week to get rid of the crutches completely—"

"Completely?" she echoed.

He looked at her ruefully. "I'm sorry. I didn't know he was keeping it a secret. He's been going along the halls here for several days getting used to being without them. I guess I assumed that since Ellie knew, the rest of you did, too. I'm sorry if I've spoiled his surprise for you."

She dismissed his apology with an impatient gesture, thinking of the questions she wanted to ask. But before she could speak, the doctor went on.

"Ellie has given your young man a lot of encouragement, but he has been good for her, too. I was the doctor when she was born, and I've seen her grow up." He shook his head. "It's a tragedy to think that so much sweetness would be wasted, squandered really, if she were to throw her life away on someone who didn't appreciate all the fine qualities she has that make up for what she lacks in some ways. I have hopes that, having met someone like your son, she will be choosy about whom she marries here."

Mrs. Andrews only half-listened, waiting to ask the questions she needed complete reassurance about.

She broke in. "Does this mean Bill is his normal self? There will be no complications, no setback?"

"None that I can foresee."

"He can return to school? Carry a full load? Do what he has always done?"

The doctor threw his hands out in a wide gesture. "I don't see any problems at all. Oh, he will have to pace himself at first. He may tire more easily than he used to and have to have an extra amount of sleep for a while. I don't advise his going out for basketball this season." He smiled at her.

Mrs. Andrews felt herself tremble as she sat back and relaxed the tight hold she had had on herself. The news was expected, dreamed of, hoped for. And yet, now that it had actually come, she had trouble believing it. The timing was so exactly right. This was Sunday. A week would take them just past Peggy's leaving, give them a day or two to get packed after she left. It would take them home in time to get Bill into school for the second semester.

She slowed her rapid thoughts and looked back at the doctor's smiling face and listened as he said, "That's quite a young man you have there. He tells me he's going to be a preacher. As far as I can tell, he already is. At least, he's been practicing on all my staff."

Mrs. Andrews stood up. "Thank you. May I tell him the news? It's not too soon?"

"Give him the good news any way you want to. Though I think he has been so sure this would be the result that he won't be surprised. Apparently with him it's not been *if* he got well, but *when*."

He rose, too, and looked at her steadily. "May I say how glad I am that it turned out this way? It doesn't always, you know, and it so easily could not have this time. As I recall, I told you in the beginning that if he recovered with no ill effects, I would consider it a miracle. We did all we could within our power, medically. And your son worked hard in every way he could. You encouraged him."

He stopped and shook his head thoughtfully. "I believe he had help from another Source as well, call it what you will."

Mrs. Andrews looked back at him for a long moment. Then she nodded at him and went out of the office and along the hall to the front door. She pulled it open and stepped out onto the wide porch. The sun shone brilliantly, warming the crisp December day.

As she stood there alone, Peggy and Bill came arm in arm, walking slowly along the wide, curving driveway, Bill's crutches hanging loose in one hand.

She watched them walk toward her and lifted one hand in a welcoming wave, her love for them flooding over her. They were the ones to whom she should turn for help, not Mrs. Withrow, not anyone else. They had the answer, had lived it before her all these years. She would ask them her question—"Peggy, Bill—how do I become a Christian?"

When she had the answer, Peggy would be able to put a check by her name on that list on the inside back page of her Bible.